Wicked Torture

"*Wanted* by J. Kenner is the whole package! A toe-curling smokin' hot read, full of incredible characters and a brilliant storyline that you won't be able to get enough of. I can't wait for the next book in this series . . . I'm hooked!"

—*Flirty & Dirty Book Blog*

"J. Kenner's evocative writing thrillingly captures the power of physical attraction, the pull of longing, the universe-altering effect one person can have on another. . . . *Claim Me* has the emotional depth to back up the sex . . . Every scene is infused with both erotic tension, and the tension of wondering what lies beneath Damien's veneer – and how and when it will be revealed."

—*Heroes and Heartbreakers*

"*Claim Me* by J. Kenner is an erotic, sexy and exciting ride. The story between Damien and Nikki is amazing and written beautifully. The intimate and detailed sex scenes will leave you fanning yourself to cool down. With the writing style of Ms. Kenner you almost feel like you are there in the story riding along the emotional rollercoaster with Damien and Nikki."

—*Fresh Fiction*

"PERFECT for fans of *Fifty Shades of Grey* and *Bared to You*. *Release Me* is a powerful and erotic romance novel that is sure to make adult romance readers sweat, sigh and swoon."

—*Reading, Eating & Dreaming Blog*

"I will admit, I am in the 'I loved *Fifty Shades*' camp, but after reading *Release Me*, Mr. Grey only scratches the surface compared to Damien Stark."

—*Cocktails and Books Blog*

"It is not often when a book is so amazingly well-written that I find it hard to even begin to accurately describe it . . . I recommend this book to everyone who is interested in a passionate love story."

—*Romancebookworm's Reviews*

"The story is one that will rank up with the *Fifty Shades* and Cross Fire trilogies."

—*Incubus Publishing Blog*

"The plot is complex, the characters engaging, and J. Kenner's passionate writing brings it all perfectly together."

—*Harlequin Junkie*

BY J. KENNER

The Stark Series:
Release Me
Claim Me
Complete Me
Anchor Me

Stark Ever After:
Take Me
Have Me
Play My Game
Seduce Me
Unwrap Me
Deepest Kiss
Entice Me
Hold Me

Stark International

Steele Trilogy:
Say My Name
On My Knees
Under My Skin
Take My Dare (includes short story Steal My Heart)

Jamie & Ryan Novellas:
Tame Me
Tempt Me

Wicked
TORTURE

J. KENNER

Wicked Torture
Copyright © 2017 by Julie Kenner

Cover design: Perfect Pear Creative Covers
Cover Photo by Kasia Bialasiewicz

ISBN: 978-1-635761-19-1

Published by Martini & Olive Books

PROLOGUE

NOTHING IN THIS *world is solid—I know that better than anyone. The way the world can suddenly shift beneath you. The way you can fight so hard and still lose everything. The way happiness can slip through your fingers.*

Luck has never been my friend. On the contrary, it has mocked and teased me, dangling happiness like a carrot that is just out of reach.

I know that—I've known it for my entire life, and it has always eluded me.

That's why I should have known better. I should have never let him get close enough to break my heart.

But I did, and now he's back.

I should have run, but he touched me, and I froze. Then he kissed me, and the world fell away.

It's wonderful.

It's terrifying.

And all I can do now is hope that he has the strength to save us both.

CHAPTER 1

S*HE HAD AN obsession with swizzle sticks.*

Noah tried to concentrate on his date's words, but it wasn't easy. She kept twisting the plastic stick between her fingers, then lifting it to her cherry red lips and teasing small drops of liquid from the end with her tongue.

He supposed that she thought it was sexy. That somehow, by stroking her tongue against the thin rod, she was making him hard.

She wasn't.

Which was probably for the best. He hadn't wanted to come out tonight, after all.

Or, correction, he hadn't wanted to come out tonight with an actual date. He'd wanted a pick-up. A one-night stand during which he could exorcise all the demons that had been roiling inside him, building up since the last time he'd let himself go. When getting lost in his work no longer had the power to battle back the memories or the guilt.

A hot, fast, intimate encounter with no strings and absolutely no purpose except the participants' mutual satisfaction. Hers, in the form of the explosive orgasm that he was more than happy to provide. His in the simple act of stepping outside of himself and away from the ghosts and the memories. Of getting lost in erotic sensations and the comfort of knowing that even though he'd destroyed two women completely, with *this* woman at least he could bring pleasure.

Correction. *Three women.* He'd destroyed *three* women.

The voice in his head was harsh. Insistent. And he winced, his body tightening as if steeling himself for a blow.

Three woman, yes. But not really. Two women, and a child.

Darla, his wife.

Kiki, his love.

And little Diana, who never even saw her first birthday. *Oh, God.*

His stomach lurched, and he fought the urge to close his eyes in defense against the memory now filling his head. His sweet Diana's lifeless body, as clear and crisp and horrible as the reality had been all those years ago.

He'd never forget—hell, he didn't want to forget.

But it had been almost nine years since Darla and Diana had been kidnapped in Mexico City, and his friends were right—he had to move on. His wife and daughter were gone, and he was here. Alive and well and trying so damn hard to block out the morass of guilt and loss, to keep it at bay with long hours of work and clandestine moments of physical release that never provided any true relief despite his continued delusions that it would help.

Which brought him right back to Evie and her swizzle stick.

"She's a lawyer based in LA, but she spends a lot of time in Austin," his friend Lyle had said when he'd insisted that Noah meet Evie for drinks. "She's pretty and smart and funny. And if it doesn't work out it's just one night out of your life. So suck it up and meet her, okay?"

Noah had wanted to say no. But he also knew it was time to start clawing his way back into the world.

So he was starting with Evie. And Lyle was right. She was smart, and she was pretty.

She might not be anonymous, but she was probably good in bed, and God knew he needed someone tonight. Needed those few moments of pure oblivion.

This week had been harder than most, and if Evie could help him forget...

He shifted in the leather armchair as he looked at her. They were tucked away in a dark corner of the bar, a small cocktail table between them. She'd stopped sucking on the swizzle stick, and now she was using it as a pointer.

"I've always loved this hotel," she said, indicating the interior of the Texas-themed bar area. The Longhorn cattle head mounted above a fireplace. The oil paintings of ranch scenes. The sofas upholstered in cowhide and leather.

Before he'd moved to Austin six months ago, he'd imagined that all of Texas resembled the inside of this bar. He'd been deeply relieved to learn he was wrong.

It was a Wednesday night, but even so, the place was crowded. The Driskill Hotel had been an Austin landmark since the 1800s, and Noah had become familiar with its restaurant, bar, and rooms during his first weeks in Austin after moving from LA. At the time, his condo was still being painted, and so he'd spent ten days in one of the suites until his own place was ready.

"It's haunted, you know," he told her.

"That's what everyone says, but I stay here every time I come from LA, and I haven't once seen a ghost. I always tell them I want one of the haunted rooms, but I never get that lucky."

"Lucky," he repeated. Considering how hard he worked to avoid the ghosts in his own life, he wasn't sure he agreed with her evaluation. "Sounds fascinating in theory, but wouldn't you be scared? Or aren't you that kind of girl?" He added the last with a tease in his voice. Because he did like her. And it wasn't her fault that she'd signed up for the deluxe Man-With-Issues package. And it really was time; he needed to start dating, not just fucking. He needed to slide back into the world.

"Scared? Oh, please." She waved a hand as if to dismiss the idea. "I'm a lawyer, remember? That's probably why I've never seen one. The ghosts run from *me* in terror."

He laughed, and she grinned, her smile lighting up the darkened bar. For a moment their eyes met and a single thought entered his head—*maybe*.

"Would you like another?" He nodded to indicate her fruity cocktail. He'd finished his own drink—two shots of bourbon, straight up—and he didn't really want another. But the air had become thick with potential, and he needed time to decide what to do about that. Dive in … or make an excuse and call it a night.

"Another drink sounds nice," she said. "And more conversation sounds even better. But the acoustics in here are tricky, and I'm starting to think this chair might be haunted, after all. I'm pretty sure I'm going to disappear into this cushion and come out in some other dimension."

Her eyes twinkled as she spoke, and he knew where she was going. What he still didn't know was if he should follow her there.

"My suite's just a few floors away," she said. "Definitely quieter. It's messy—I have depositions spread out all over the coffee table. But the couch is comfortable and there's a wet bar that's nicely stocked…"

She trailed off with a small shrug of invitation.

"And you don't have anywhere to be tomorrow morning," he pointed out, remembering what she'd said when they'd spoken that afternoon. Her case had settled during the lunch break when the plaintiff she'd been examining decided that he wasn't feeling litigious after all. Suddenly, she not only had this night free, but most of tomorrow as well, since she'd been unable to change her evening flight back to Los Angeles.

"True," she said, tugging her purse up to her lap as if in preparation to leave. "We can talk all night if you want. Or not talk," she added boldly, as if he could have misinterpreted the direction of this conversation.

"There is a certain virtue in silence." He kept his tone light. Flirtatious. But inside he was still debating.

Lyle's voice seemed to fill his head. *I'm not saying you need to marry her. But put yourself out there. Interact with the world. Start breathing again, man. Trust me. It's worth it."*

Of course, Lyle would think so. Like Noah, Lyle had closed himself off from anything resembling a real relationship. But that was before Sugar Laine walked into his life. Now, Lyle was the happiest that Noah had ever seen him, and Noah knew that had everything to do with Sugar.

Noah wasn't Lyle, but maybe his friend was right. And, honestly, Noah had known for months—hell, maybe years—that it was time to move on. Time to stop with the quick and dirty encounters that did nothing to dull his pain.

Time to heal.

Somehow, though, he never found the enthusiasm. Or maybe that was just an excuse. Another way of punishing himself for walking away from the woman he loved in favor of the woman he'd owed.

And since he'd never have either of them again, he needed to kick his own ass, pick up the pieces of his life, and start building something real. After all, there wasn't a tech gadget he couldn't design, build, or repair. So why was he so clueless when it came to his own damn life?

It was time, and it would be easy. Painless even, because God knew Evie embodied everything he admired in a woman. Strength. Intelligence. Ambition. Humor. Beauty. She was as desirable as Lyle had promised and obviously enthusiastic.

In other words, he was all out of excuses.

He stood up, intending to tell her to lead the way. But the words that came out of his mouth shocked them both. "I'm sorry, Evie," he said. "You've been wonder-

7

ful, but I have an early meeting, and I should probably get home."

"Oh." He'd surprised her as she was rising, and now she teetered awkwardly on her heels, as if his unexpected words would physically topple her.

He reached out a hand to steady her, and for the briefest moment, he considered pulling her close and fighting his way past his hesitation. She was everything he should want in a woman—with the unfortunately insurmountable problem that she wasn't what he wanted at all. Or, rather, she wasn't *who* he wanted.

Goddamn him.

Goddamn his stupid, unrealistic fantasies.

And while he was at it, goddamn Kiki, too.

He was being an idiot and unfair, and he knew it. An idiot, because he'd made his choice to walk away from Kiki long ago, and he knew damn well that he'd shattered her in the process. Even if he could have seen his way clear to look her up after all these years, he'd forfeited his right to come crawling back.

Unfair, because not ten minutes ago he'd been ready to take the plunge with Evie, and yet here he was, dodging and shifting like a damn coward, trying to swim up out of the deep black ocean of loss and pain. A familiar pain that wrapped him like a blanket, so cloying it was almost comfortable. And he knew damn well that there was only one way to fight it—he needed to take the girl to her room and try to fuck the darkness out of him.

The way he'd done with countless other women.

The way that never worked like it should. That only dulled the sharp edges of his pain, but added no light to the darkness.

That wasn't what he wanted. Not anymore. One of the reasons he'd moved to Austin was to heal, after all. To heal, and to break bad habits.

Still, it was tempting, and it took more strength than he expected to shake his head again and say very gently, "I really am sorry. I'm not … ready." She'd been polite enough not to mention the tragedy in his past, but he was certain that Lyle must have at least told her that he'd lost his wife and daughter. Hopefully, that softened the blow of rejection.

She'd regained her footing, and now she stepped back, her forehead creased as her eyes flicked over him, expertly assessing him as she would a witness. "It's been almost nine years, I'm told." The sharp edge of her voice sliced his heart. So much for softening the blow. "If you don't get ready soon, I can't help but think you're going to end up sad and alone."

With a thin, sympathetic smile, she turned and walked away, leaving him to watch her go and wonder at her perceptiveness. Because she was right.

He was going to end up sad and alone.

Hell, he already was.

BUILT MORE OR less in the shape of a rectangle, the hotel spanned most of a city block, with entrances on each of the three sides that abutted a street.

Usually when Noah grabbed a drink at The Driskill, he left through the bar entrance and emerged onto

Seventh Street. From there, he could walk the partial block to Congress Avenue, the main downtown artery. He'd head south, checking his phone for messages and putting out fires as he maneuvered the short distance home. A few blocks before the river, he'd hook a right, enter his building through the Third Street entrance, and take the elevator up to the fifteenth floor and the studio he'd bought when he'd moved to Austin earlier in the year.

At the time, he'd considered getting a bigger place—God knew he could afford it—but what would be the point? He was rarely at home. His work was his life, just as it had been for years. And frankly, the only reason he ever bothered to come to the condo at all was because it disconcerted the janitorial staff when he slept on the couch in his office.

Besides, when he'd looked at the building, all the available larger condos had views of the Capital building. He preferred the smaller space and its stunning view of the river. Every morning he watched the walkers and joggers. The kayaks and paddleboats. The infinite shades of green that lined the river's wide banks, then burst into color when the peach blossoms bloomed, shifting the usually green-tinted vista to a vivid pink.

It was vibrant. Alive.

Hopeful, even.

He'd set up his desk in front of the window, and on weekends, he was training himself to work from home. He'd sit at the desk and draw schematics or scribble notes while he watched the activity below. Parents pushing strollers as they walked lazily down the paths.

Children tottering on bicycles, obviously fresh out of training wheels. Joggers, determined to lose those extra five pounds. Lovers walking arm in arm, deep in conversation.

There was a never-ending stream of life fifteen stories below him. And the more Noah looked at it, the more he was starting to believe that maybe one day he could rejoin that current.

Maybe.

But not now. Not tonight.

Besides, it was dark. If he went home now, he'd only see the reflection of the moon on the still water. Beautiful, yes. But also surreal and far too lonely.

All of which was why he didn't leave the hotel through the bar, as usual. Instead, he took the stairs down to The Driskill's ornate lobby, then crossed over the marble floor to the main entrance. A doorman hurried to pull the heavy wood and glass door open for him, and a valet nodded speculatively, expecting a ticket. Noah shook his head to indicate that he had no car, then shoved his hands into his jacket pockets as he turned right and walked the short distance to the corner.

He'd learned that Austin rarely got too cold, but right now there was a definite chill in the air, which he relished. Although he'd lived most of his life in Southern California, he'd enjoyed his time in New York, especially the changing seasons, and it was nice to be able to pretend that Thanksgiving and Christmas might come with at least a drop in temperature, if not Autumn colors and snow.

He crossed the street at the corner, and then hesitated. Turn right, and he could be home in less than ten minutes. Turn left, and he'd invariably find himself in a bar, and the evening would end with him either alone and feeling sorry for himself, or with him in a hotel room, creeping out before dawn while a woman whose name he couldn't remember slept soundly in a rented bed.

He turned left.

He had no specific intent, but he couldn't bear the loneliness of his own studio. For a moment, he considered texting Evie. Apologizing. Asking if she wanted to meet at one of the nearby bars. He dismissed the idea, afraid that she'd say no. Or, worse, that she'd say yes.

Instead he just walked, pausing briefly in front of Maggie Mae's, a local establishment that long-time Austinites told him had been a Sixth Street fixture for decades.

He considered going in, but he could hear the intense beat of the live music even from where he stood on the sidewalk. And when he peered through the windows, it was obvious that finding a seat would be damn near impossible, much less squeezing in to sidle up to the bar.

Some nights, it would be worth it, just to get lost in the rhythm of the music and drown out the noise in his head.

Tonight, he wanted to be able to hear his own thoughts, though he wasn't sure why. He might have the skill and intellect to have turned the balance sheet of the new Austin division of Stark Applied Technology around in under a year, but outside the realm of business and tech, the inside of his head remained a morass of regret and longing and confusion.

Frankly, he was getting damn tired of it.

He continued until he reached The Fix on Sixth, another local staple. The drinks were excellent and the bar food put every other joint on the street to shame. He'd heard a few rumors that the place might close, though he had no idea why, and he hoped it wasn't true. He liked the place, and the owner, Tyree, always remembered his name.

Tonight, The Fix looked to be in no danger of going out of business. Even on a Wednesday, he had to push his way through the crowd that clustered near a wooden stage bordered by two walls of windows that gave a view of the corner intersection and the pedestrians and cars humming about outside. There was no performer, not yet, but a man Noah recognized as one of the bartenders was adjusting the height of a microphone in front of a single metal stool.

On any other night, Noah might have stayed to listen. Right now, he wanted to escape the crowd.

He wound his way through the throng, passing the long bar that extended deep into the room as he made his way to the smaller—and blissfully quieter—bar area in the back.

From behind this secluded bar, Tyree waved a greeting. A large black man with broad shoulders and arms as thick as a woman's thigh, he was often mistaken for the bouncer rather than the owner of The Fix. He was, however, more suited for the latter. Tyree had some of the kindest eyes that Noah had ever seen, and an easy-going manner that wasn't suited for tossing rowdy patrons out on their asses.

"What's your poison, Noah?" he asked after passing something fruity to one of two college girls sitting at the bar. Their blonde heads were bent close together, and Noah could almost make out words as they alternated whispers with stolen glances at the second bartender behind the rail, who seemed unaware of them as he expertly mixed the Manhattan that Noah had requested.

"Are you new?" Noah asked. "You look familiar, but I'm not sure why."

"I've been here a few months," he said, wiping his hands on a bar rag. "But I just started working a regular night shift yesterday. Before, I filled in at night or covered lunch. I'm Cam, by the way."

"Cam's a grad student at UT," Tyree explained as Noah frowned, still trying to place him. He studied the guy's face—young, but not naive, with intelligent blue-gray eyes, dark brown hair, and a single earring—and tried to remember where he'd seen it before.

He shook his head, still pulling a blank. "What are you studying?" Maybe that would jar his memory. Noah was certain he'd met the guy before, and his inability to place the kid was bothering him more than it should.

If Cam answered, though, Noah didn't hear it, because at that moment, there was a lull in the din filtering in from the front room, then a smattering of applause before a male voice announced that there was a pre-show surprise. A local performer he hoped they enjoyed.

Noah tuned it out. When he was younger, he'd loved live music. Now, it just brought back unwelcome memories.

He glanced at Tyree. "I didn't think you brought bands in on Wednesdays."

"Usually don't. This one's getting quite a local following, though, and they leave soon on a three-state tour. The lead singer asked if they could do a farewell performance." A wide grin lit his face. "Honestly, I think he mostly wanted his girlfriend to have the chance to try out her new song on a live audience. She's not part of the band, but she's got chops."

"She's not his—" Cam began, but Noah wasn't listening anymore. Because the voice from the front room had reached him, low and clear and hauntingly familiar.

It couldn't be. Could it?

He stood, then moved to the doorway that separated the two areas. He squeezed in between patrons knotted in tight groups, the words seeming to pull him closer even as the voice made him want to draw away.

"...and when I'm feeling blue, I always circle back to you..."

He didn't hear anymore. How could he now that he was looking at her? Now that the wild roar of emotion and memory was filling his head?

Now that he was staring at the woman he'd loved.

The woman he'd destroyed.

And the woman whose voice was even now tearing his heart into pieces.

CHAPTER 2

"...I LOSE MYSELF in sorrow, clinging to tomorrow.
   I don't know how I will get through..."

The words soar out of me, my chest swelling as emotion fills my heart. And not just the emotion of the song, but the knowledge that I'm back.

This song—the first one I've performed in almost ten years—isn't just good, it *works*.

I can see it on the ardent faces in the audience. The bodies held tight with anticipation, as if the music is a tangible thing that they can cling to, letting it carry them away to another world.

I've nailed it. And the pride inside me is laced with relief as sweet and warm as fudge sauce on vanilla ice cream.

I'm back. I'm finally back.

My voice rises as the music and lyrics tell the story. Her triumph over the memory of him. The way she claims her victory by reclaiming her life.

She survived, tall and proud and ready to shut the door on the past and finally move on.

That's the song, anyway.

The reality goes deeper. The reality is that *I* survived.

And I lived to sing about it.

I'm performing only this one song tonight, but when it ends, I'm utterly drained. I've thrown everything I have into it—emotion, memory, regrets, ambitions—and as the audience clusters around me, I'm almost afraid I won't be able to stand when I slide off this stool.

But their applause restores me, just the way it used to. I feel my strength returning, and I plant my feet on the stage, then casually hand my guitar to Ares when he strides over, his hand extended, so that I can take a bow. Which I do, relishing the moment.

"What do you say, folks?" Ares asks. "Is this girl back or is she back?"

A general cheer rises from the crowd, and I laugh, delighted. I've never shied from an audience, and now I smile at the faces near me, silently thanking them all for giving me a chance. After all, they'd come tonight to hear Ares and his band, Seven Percent, before they leave Austin to head out on tour. My performance could have been an annoyance.

"Kiki King, ladies and gentlemen," Ares goes on, as I continue to scope out the crowd. "In case you didn't know it, she was one of the founding members of Pink Chameleon, and wrote their biggest hit, *Turnstile*."

He doesn't mention that *Turnstile* was the last song I both wrote and recorded, and I'm grateful for his oversight. Anyone in the audience who's familiar with Pink Chameleon probably knows that I left the band and dropped out of the music scene while *Turnstile* was still climbing the charts, even if they don't know why.

The rest of them only know what they just heard.

And since I'm starting over, that's more than enough.

I take another bow at Ares' urging and then look out at the crowd again. They're still clapping, and I'm still basking. And as I look past the nearby faces, I see my little brother Cameron standing in the doorway that leads to the smaller bar in the back.

He's clapping wildly, and I roll my eyes when he thrusts two fingers into his mouth and releases a wolf whistle that carries over the din all the way to where I'm standing on the stage. My smile spreads wide, then I laugh out loud when his boss, Tyree, steps up behind him and glares down until Cam notices, shoots me an apologetic glance, then hurries back to serve drinks or chat up patrons or whatever other bar-related duty he's been shirking.

Tyree lingers, and though he tries hard to look fierce, I see the pride in his eyes as he nods at me, and my overfull heart swells a little bit more.

I'd found Cam so easily in the back of the room that I hadn't noticed any of the other patrons standing near him. But now, as I'm about to take a sideways step toward Ares, I catch a glimpse of red hair in a shade so familiar it makes my heart ache.

It can't be him. He's just on my mind, that's all. The man I once loved. The son-of-a-bitch who'd inspired tonight's song.

But no way is he really here, and I'm still repeating that mantra when he lifts his chin, I see his eyes, and the world starts to fall out from under me.

No.

No, it's my imagination. The song. The music. My

mind playing tricks on me.

It's not him. It can't be. Why would he be here? In Austin? In this bar? On this night?

Panic flutters inside me, hot and wild. I've just gotten my shit together. Just started writing again, singing again. I have a plan, a whole map for the rest of my life, and I don't want to see Noah Carter at all.

And the sky is pink, rainclouds are full of wine, and ice cream has negative calories.

I start to search the crowd, looking for another glimpse of that familiar burnished copper. But then Ares calls to me, and I realize that Seven Percent is ready to start their set. Reluctantly, I wave a final goodbye to the crowd, then hug Ares before hurrying off the stage. I know I should linger and listen to them—either that or just get the hell out of The Fix—but like a good little masochist, I push away from the stage and deeper into the bar, right straight toward where I saw Noah. Or, I'm hoping, the Noah-like apparition.

I'm ground level now, and I can't see much of anything. I'm five-seven only when I'm in heels, and today I'm wearing canvas flats, which means my view consists primarily of a sea of male chests.

I nip through the crowd, shifting and turning as I work my way backward. It's slow going. Not only do more than a few people pause to tell me they enjoyed my performance, but I'm also stymied by the fact that most folks are moving toward the stage at the front of the bar, which means that I'm fighting against the current.

I tell myself I should go home. My mind is playing tricks, and I need to get out of here. Except I can't seem to make my feet cooperate, and they lead me inexorably forward. I'm not sure what I expect to find when I finally push through the crowd—a tall man with red hair and nothing else familiar about him? Or the man I'd once loved with all my heart and soul?

More important, I'm not sure what I want to find.

The question, however, is moot. By the time I get to the doorframe that marks the entrance to the quieter back bar, Noah's nowhere to be seen.

If it even was Noah. Which, of course, it wasn't.

I squeeze past two frat boys whose broad shoulders seem to fill the doorway, then peer around the room, my pulse pounding so noisily I can barely hear the strains of Seven Percent's first song behind me.

He isn't here.

Neither Noah, nor anyone who looks like him.

Had my imagination been playing tricks? Or had we passed in the crowd, him going one way and me the other?

I shift my attention to the area behind the bar, searching for Cam. But he's not there either. Not that he could have confirmed that the man with red hair was Noah. Cam's ten years younger than me, and even though I showed Noah pictures of my brother and bragged repeatedly, the two never actually met.

Which leaves me standing like an idiot in the doorway, my forehead creased into a scowl.

"Considering you blew them away in there, you don't look very happy."

I glance to my left, where Tyree is standing at a table chatting up two guys in business suits who I assume are regulars. Immediately, my mood shifts, and I smile.

"Thank you so much for letting me go on before Seven Percent," I say, genuinely grateful. "I know Ares tossed the idea at you out of left field yesterday, and even though it was only me with a microphone and my guitar, I understand what a hassle last minute changes can be, so I—"

He holds up a hand to cut off my flow of words. "I was happy to do it. Hell, I'm glad you took us up on the opportunity."

My smile wavers a little, and I wonder how much Ares told him. We've been friends since college, when we both attended the University of Texas. I whizzed through in three years, mostly because I was bored with school and wanted to perform, and I left for Los Angeles while Ares stayed behind in Austin.

He introduced me to his LA-based cousin Celia, though, and she and I ended up forming Pink Chameleon with two other girls.

When I moved back to Austin, I looked him up, of course, and he was a solid rock in my personal post-Noah storm. He's one of the few people who knows that I'm on the edge of the springboard, my toes curling over as I steady myself, gathering my courage to leap off the high dive and back into my dream of a career in music.

More than that, he's one of only a handful who understands how much I've had to heal so I could claw my way up to that sky-high platform in the first place.

I hug myself. Seeing Noah could destroy all of that. Hell, just thinking about Noah could set me back.

But only if I let it.

I straighten my shoulders, remembering everything I've gone through. How much I've sacrificed and how hard I've worked. And you know what? Fuck Noah.

Fuck him and his maybe-here, maybe-not apparition. I can handle the man, and I can handle his ghost. And I'm sure as hell not going to run scared.

Not only that, but if he is here, I want to know why. And if he's intentionally playing peek-a-boo, I want to know why even more. Austin's my place now. My safe spot. It's where I'd run to escape the memory of him—of *us*.

It's the place that sheltered and healed me. That gave me the strength to build a wall around the pain. Then helped me to shut those sweet memories up behind it. The precious memories that ached deep inside, and gave the pain both fire and the steel-honed edge of a razor.

He can't be here. Because if he's here, I'm not sure that I can keep those walls from crumbling down.

For a moment, I consider turning around and leaving. I should just go home, go to sleep, and pretend like this night ended with the crowd's applause. After all, I still have a ton of preparation to do for tomorrow's crucial pitch meeting. Because the sad truth is, music may be my first love, but marketing pays the bills.

Besides, the odds are it wasn't him. Because why on earth would he even be here?

Then again, I don't know where else he should be. I've taken a lot of pains to avoid learning anything at all about Noah Carter over the years, and as far as my world is concerned, he doesn't exist.

Except maybe he does.

I know the odds are slim, but I also know that even if I went home, I wouldn't sleep. I'd obsess.

And so I draw a breath for courage and then walk the short distance to the bar. Tyree's behind it again, and I perch on the only unoccupied stool.

"Chardonnay?"

I shake my head. "Just a question. Did you happen to see a guy in here earlier. Tall. Amazing green eyes. Good looking, but it sneaks up on you." I bite back a smile, remembering the first time I'd seen Noah. He'd been working on a video game that I was scoring. I'd been told I needed to talk to him, and that he was in the last cubicle. I'd found him hunched over his keyboard, his eyes heavy from lack of sleep, his hair sticking up in all directions.

He'd glanced up at me, and I'd barely noticed. Then he'd stood, his hand smoothing down his hair before he smiled—and it was as if a spotlight had suddenly been aimed at him. I took it all in. His muscled arms. His broad chest. The eleven-plus inches he surely had on me. A strong face with a wide mouth and honest eyes. And thick, unruly hair that suggested a carefree attitude in a man who turned out to have the kind of killer work ethic I admire. Who was, in fact, the owner of the company, even though he worked out of that cramped, crappy space.

His smile slayed me, wide and bright and filled with genuine humor. But it was his eyes that stole my heart. The connection that sparked in them the moment our gazes locked. The silent greeting of one soul to another when the only thing that needs to be said is, *I know you.*

Or, at least, I'd known him back then. I thought I had, anyway.

I give myself a mental shake, realizing I hadn't told Tyree the most pertinent detail. "And he has red hair. Copper-colored, really. I saw him standing in the door-way when I was on stage, and I think he's a guy I knew in Los Angeles." I try to sound casual. "Did you notice anyone like that?"

"Sure," Tyree says, as if my question had no weight at all. As if his answer doesn't have the ability to strike a physical blow. "You must be looking for Noah Carter."

CHAPTER 3

I STAND ON the sidewalk, my thoughts in a muddle. I barely remember leaving The Fix, but I'm sure I thanked Tyree for telling me about Noah. After that, I must have pushed through the crowded bar, then burst through the doors onto Sixth Street.

And that's where I am now. Standing in the middle of a sidewalk jammed with pedestrians and wondering how I got here ... and more important, where I intend to go next.

That's not to say I remember nothing. Quite the contrary. I remember Tyree telling me that the ginger-haired man was Noah, then explaining that he knows the man's name because Noah's been coming in every week or so for the last couple of months, and when a man frequents your establishment, it's good to at least learn his name.

What he didn't know was where Noah went, other than to say that he'd exited out the back. "Said he didn't want to deal with pushing through the throng around Ares and his boys," Tyree had said. "I told him to use the service entrance and to leave through the alley. You can probably catch him if you go that way, too."

I'd shaken my head so hard and fast it's a wonder my

eyeballs didn't rattle. "No. No, I was just wondering if that was him. I'm sure I'll see him around. I'm going … I'll just…"

I hooked my thumb over my shoulder to indicate the front. After that, I must have followed my thumb, although I don't remember my feet moving. All I remember is the noise in my head. Desire mixed with anger. Fury bolstered by memory.

Noah had been my heart—hell, he'd been my muse. And when he'd walked away from me, the world beneath my feet had cracked like ice on a winter pond, the fissures radiating in all directions, destroying everything and sending me tumbling into someplace dark and cold and lonely.

It took me years to claw my way back out. To thaw enough to even pick up my guitar again. But I did, and now I'm finally starting to breathe new life into dreams that I thought had died when he left.

I got over him, dammit. I built a new life in a new city, and how dare he come here and ruin all of that.

It's probably innocent. A coincidence.

After all, Austin is a tech town, and Noah has always been a tech guy. Maybe he's just here for work.

Maybe he was as surprised to see me as I was to see him.

I don't know, and the reason I don't know is that the goddamn coward up and left without even talking to me. At least in Los Angeles he had the balls to say goodbye. This time he just slinked out into the dark.

Motherfucker.

Before, I didn't follow him. I hadn't fought; I'd just

let him go. That's what people do, after all. They leave. Everybody leaves.

I'd fooled myself into believing that Noah would stay, and I'd paid a hefty price for my mistake.

But it's a price I can't afford anymore. I need him gone. I need my head clear.

I have to protect my muse; I have to protect my heart.

And I sure as hell can't handle the thought that at any place and at any time he could pop into my life like a Noah-shaped Whack-a-Mole to tempt and tease, and then just walk away all over again.

All of which adds up to one simple conclusion—I need to put on my big girl panties, catch up with him, and find out why the hell he's here.

Shit.

I round the corner at a clip, walk the length of the bar, then turn right into the alley. I'm irritated with myself for having lingered on the sidewalk. Or, for that matter, not following him out the back door as Tyree had suggested.

Time's been ticking away, and Noah's surely gone. Which means I'm going to be on edge from now until forever, seeing him in every crowd, expecting him around every corner.

Damn him. Damn him for getting under my skin even after all these years.

I feel tears sting my eyes, and I clench my fists at my sides as I stride deeper into the alley, fighting the stress and the sadness and the whole confusing miasma of emotions swirling around inside of me.

It's dark back here, and the air is putrid from too little wind and too much rotten food tossed out behind the various restaurants and bars. My stomach twists, and I concentrate on watching my step, which is harder than it sounds since the alley is so dim, the only illumination provided by the few anorexic lights marking the various establishments' back doors.

I pass the rear entrance to The Fix and continue heading west, picking up speed as I do. Not just because I'm hoping to catch up with Noah, but because I know how foolish it is to be back in this alley at night, especially with all the dark nooks and shadowed crannies. Formerly Pecan Street, this section of Sixth Street has been a commercial center of the town since the late 1800s. An intriguing bit of history, sure, but right now I'm thinking more about the construction of these buildings. About how the back walls don't quite line up, so that there are deep, shadowed insets along the path.

And here I am, strolling through those shadows like an idiot. I might as well be wearing an *Attackers welcome!* sign on my ass.

I hear a clatter behind me, and spin around in time to see a mangy orange cat streak behind a trash bin. I bend over to catch my breath, shocked at how hard my pulse is pounding and how loud the roar of blood is in my ears. I'm on edge, plain and simple, and if I were smart, I'd give it up, go home, and worry about Noah Carter tomorrow.

Or never. Never would be even better.

It's a good plan. A sane plan. And I stand up straight, fully intending to shed my momentary foolishness and walk back the way I came. Then I can cut diagonally to the lot where I parked my car, go home, and fall into blissful oblivion until my alarm clock wakes me at six, and I dive into prep for my afternoon meeting.

Having made what I consider the wise decision, I take a single step forward. But that's as far as I get. Because the moment I take the second step, the shadows on my left shift, and before my mind even has time to tell my mouth to scream, Noah is standing in front of me.

My heart twists as my brain catches up to reality. *It really is him.*

Even in the dark, I can see the planes and angles of his face, the strength of his jaw. His wide mouth, usually curved up in humor, but right now set in a thin line that suggests a frown.

He's only a few feet away, but the distance between us is vast. He moves tentatively toward me, as if mere proximity can somehow breech the gap. It can't, of course. But though I want to back away—to regain my ability to think rational thoughts—my feet seem glued to the asphalt. I'm trapped here, as enchanted as if I was a princess in a fairy tale.

"Kiki," he says, and the sound of my name on his lips breaks the spell. Before I even realize what I'm doing, I raise my hand and slap him hard across the face.

I gasp. Not from the pain—though my palm does sting—but from the shock of what I've done. I stand frozen, my hand still only inches from his face, as my mind churns with indecision. Do I apologize? Or do I tell him that he deserved the slap, and I hope his face stings just as much as my hand?

But it's all happening too fast, and I don't have time to reach a decision before he catches my wrist and yanks me toward him so quickly that I let out an involuntary yelp.

"Dammit, Noah, let me go. We both know you deserved that."

He's pulled me close, so that my arm is bent at the elbow, my upper arm pressed against my chest. His hand is still closed around my wrist, and because of the way he's holding me, his fingers brush against the V-neck of my T-shirt, as well as a bit of bare skin.

My head is tilted back, and he's looking right at my face. I have no idea if he realizes how intimate his touch is. But it doesn't matter. *I* realize it, and the more I try not to focus on the way his skin feels against mine, the more I find it difficult to focus on anything else at all.

"I do deserve it," he says agreeably, "but don't even think about doing it again."

"Then let me go," I snap. "Or are you going to hold me here all night just so you can protect your stupid face?" I glance down. I sound ridiculous, and I know it, and I have no desire to see amusement in his eyes.

I want to sound clever and sharp and righteous. But I can't seem to conjure the words. Hell, I can't seem to concentrate on anything except the way his skin feels against mine. Just the tiniest of touches, and yet it is both wildly obvious and disturbingly intimate. And to make it worse, my heart is beating so fast and so hard that I'm sure he can tell. More than that, I'm sure he realizes he's the reason.

The thought gives me strength, and I jerk myself free, then step back. It's only a few inches, but it does me a world of good. I can practically feel common sense flooding back into me. "Why are you here?" I demand.

"I'm working in Austin now," he says. "I'm heading up a division at—"

"Not *here*," I say, waving my hand to encompass the entire town. I'm irritated by his easy answer. By the fact that he doesn't seem to be rattled at all, and I'm close to losing it. "*Here*. In this alley. Behind The Fix. Why are you lurking back here instead of inside talking to me like any sane man would be doing? Why did you scurry out the back door like you'd walked into a nightmare and couldn't wait to get away from a demon that haunts you?"

I take another step back, then realize that my cheeks are wet. I hadn't meant for all of that to spill out of me any more than I'd meant to cry. "Dammit," I say as I scrub my palms over my face.

"Here." He pulls a handkerchief out of his pocket and hands it to me. "It's clean," he adds with a ghost of a smile.

"Of course it is." I take it gratefully, then dab my eyes, wishing I didn't care that I now probably look like a raccoon. Because why should I care what I look like around Noah?

I draw a breath. "Thanks."

"Any time," he says, and this time the smile is more than a ghost. There's a definite up-curve to his lips, and I have to work to fight my own smile. Because Noah Carter wasn't a handkerchief-carrying kind of guy until he met me. But I've always been a crier. Not in a bad way, just in all the ways. I cry at happy movies; I cry at sad movies. I cry at sentimental commercials. And, sometimes, I even cry at the stupid ones.

Honestly, it's a wonder I ever manage to get a song down on paper, because while I'm composing, I can barely see through the tears.

About the only time I don't cry is when I'm performing. Then, the emotion comes out through my voice, not my tear ducts.

Now the smile has reached his eyes, and I bite back a laugh. That's how it always was with us. One minute I'd be sniffling over something sentimental, the next minute we'd be laughing and racing down the beach, hand in hand, until we fell together in the surf, lost in the wonder that was each other and the world.

With Noah, the world was always wide and wonderful, beautiful and mysterious. Mostly, though, it was full of delight. He could make a drive to the grocery store as much of an adventure as a hike in the mountains.

"You still carry them," I say, passing it back to him.

He nods, then tucks it back into his pocket without quite meeting my eyes. My stomach twists, and I wish I hadn't said anything. Now I'm picturing him passing one to his wife as they sit in a darkened theater watching a sappy movie. Or wiping the nose of a small child. A little boy, maybe, who's fallen and scraped his knee, but is trying so hard to be brave.

They're the ones he laughs with now.

I swallow, fighting back another wave of tears. And this time, I'm determined not to cry. Not for him. Not for us.

Because I'm over him. I got over him a long time ago.

That's what I tell myself, anyway. But I know it's bullshit. I'm not over him. I'll probably never be over him.

But I have moved on. And his sudden appearance is like a rope tied tight around my ankles dragging me back into the past.

"So?" I demand, realizing he never answered my question. "Why are you lurking in alleys?"

He slides both hands through his hair, then interlocks his fingers on top of his head. I've seen him do the same thing hundreds of times, usually in front of a computer when he's frustrated by some uncooperative bit of coding.

Right now, I guess I'm the uncooperative one.

"I wasn't trying to upset you," he says. "Honestly, I thought I was making it easier."

"Easier?" A fresh burst of anger cuts through me, and my brow rises along with my temper. "Easier than what? Than you tossing me aside for another woman? Easier than a punch in the gut? Maybe it's been easy for you, Noah, but you put me through hell."

"I didn't—"

"*No.*" I hold up a hand. "Screw your apologies and your excuses. I'm over it," I say. "Over. Done. All healed up. And you do not—repeat, *not*—get to just waltz back into my life and send me reeling. This is my town now. My life. And you need to either get the hell out or stay the hell out of my way. Do you under—"

"Kiki?" I hear Cam's voice simultaneously with the squeak of metal hinges. "Hey, are you out here?"

I freeze, and Noah stares at me. I must look spooked, because his brow creases with worry.

What? he mouths.

My brother, I reply, equally silent. They've never met, but of course Cam knows about my past drama with Noah. And right now really isn't the time to bring my brother into the morass of *Noah & Kiki: The Sequel.*

Thankfully, I see comprehension on Noah's face. He presses his palms to my shoulders and eases me deeper into the shadows, step by step, until we're tucked into one of the indentations made from the intersection of two semi-connected buildings.

"What the hell, Cam?" It's a female voice, and one I don't recognize.

"I heard someone yell, and then I thought I heard my sister. *Kiki!*" he calls again, and Noah touches his fingertip to my lips, as if I'd be stupid enough to respond.

I want to glare at him, but it's impossible. I can't do anything but stand frozen, hoping he doesn't feel the renewed tension in my body. Hoping that the heat from his finger doesn't singe my lips, and that he can't feel the way my breathing has changed. How I'm suddenly aware of my skin, of his touch.

I swallow, and pray that he thinks my nervousness is because of Cam.

His eyes are locked on mine, and I can see the warning in them. The silent admonishment to remain still, as if we were nothing more than shadows ourselves.

But there's heat there, too. I know him too well not to recognize the tension behind his eyes, and to understand what it means. Memories of long nights and intimate touches. Of soft words and broken promises.

I release a shuddering sigh, a mixture of both longing and regret.

"There's no one out here," the girl says. "And I saw her go out the front, anyway."

"Weird." I can image Cam's frown. I can't see his face, but from the shadows, I can see him emerge from behind the open door. His posture is stiff. Worried. There's no reason to be worried, of course, but we've always been close. Our grandmother used to say that except for the ten years between us—and the fact that we're half-siblings—we were practically twins. So his concern doesn't surprise me at all, and I fear that he's going to move further down the alley, checking out the nooks and crannies just to be on the safe side.

"Cam?" I hear Tyree's low, booming voice.

"He's here!" the girl calls, then adds in a lower voice. "Go back in. If it's bugging you so much I'll take a quick look around."

They both step behind the open door and out of my line of sight. There's a low murmur of conversation that I can't hear, and then the door shuts. Cam is gone, but I can see the outline of the girl as she steps away from the door and into the alley.

She turns toward us, and Noah steps forward, the hand at my mouth moving to my hip as he steers me even further back until I feel my body pressed against the cool brick of the building behind me.

"Quiet," he whispers as her heels click on the concrete.

I raise a brow, annoyed. I hardly need reminding.

But then he steps closer, and I gasp audibly. He catches me with a sharp glance, and I point up, indicating his hair.

For a moment, he frowns, apparently confused. Then he looks up, and notices what I've just realized—that as we'd moved further into this alcove, we'd passed through a sliver of light from a nearby fixture. The beam has hit Noah's hair, making it spark and shine.

He takes one more step toward me, so that we are both in this tiny, shadowed space. Now, instead of merely his finger on my lips or his hands on my shoulders, his entire body is flush against mine, one hand on the wall behind me for balance. I want to tell him to lean back, but we both know that would put him in the light. And all my plea would do is tell him that his proximity is making me nervous. Which he probably already knows.

Nervous and, damn me, far too aware of every touch. Every breath.

My palm is flat against his chest, though I don't remember lifting it. I can feel the tempo of his heart, and am relieved to find that it's galloping, just like my own. My eyes are aligned with his neck, and even in the dark I can see the curve of it rising to a strong jaw that my lips have traced so many times. It's been years, but I can still imagine the feel of his skin against my mouth, the rough sensuality of his beard stubble against my lips, my cheeks.

I close my eyes, trying to ward off the memories, then open them again when I hear the woman's footsteps draw near.

Noah leans in, his hips pressing against my lower abs as he uses his entire body to shield me. If the girl sees anything, it will look like a couple grabbing some alone time in a dark corner. Either that, or a drunken man all by himself. I have no clue if I'm even visible at all.

I hold my breath, hyperaware of the sound of her passing, and even more aware of the feel of Noah's body against mine. I tilt my head up, and his face is right there, his lips parted, the scent of whiskey on his breath. His eyes are on mine, and time melts away.

I don't know how long we stand like that, breathing each other's air, seeing each other's thoughts. It seems no longer than an instant; it seems like forever.

Neither of us moves, and after a moment, I hear the clink of the door shutting as the girl goes back inside. But still, we stay frozen, as if we both have one foot in the past, and if we so much as blink, the spell will be broken.

Then his head tilts. It's barely even the hint of a movement, but it's enough. I straighten, knowing I need to push past him. But before I can move, his mouth closes over mine.

I freeze. I'm flat against the wall, completely trapped. Some small part of me wants to push him back—my hand is already on his chest. It would be so easy to do. But I can't—I won't. And soon that tiny seed of rationality is swallowed up by need and want and greed.

It's as if I've been starving, and Noah is the finest chocolate, the most tempting liquor. I want to savor him, but I can't resist. I clutch him tight, matching his heat, his need. His mouth is hard and demanding against mine, as if he's trying to consume me, to draw me in, to claim me completely. And so help me, I want that. In this moment, I don't care about the past or my anger or my hurt. All I want is to recapture what we had. All I want is the man I once knew and that touch, that passion, so all-consuming. So combustible.

So goddamn dangerous.

The thought hits me hard, and I push away from him, gasping with shock, my skin hot from a mixture of lust and self-loathing. I'd been drawn into the past, all right. A past when things were good. When I'd let myself believe we had a future.

But that wasn't how the story ended, and I shouldn't have let myself block out reality any more than I should have let him kiss me. Because in the real past, he left me.

In the real past, he walked away so that he could marry someone else.

"Kiki, I'm sorry. I—"

"Just go," I snap, as fresh tears prick my eyes. "Just go back to your wife."

He flinches, and I expect him to say something. To make some excuse.

But he doesn't. He just backs away from me, and as he passes under the light, I can see his expression. Hurt. Confusion. And something I can't quite identify.

He's in the middle of the alley when he speaks again, his face lost in the shadows. "I really am sorry," he says as he starts to walk away. "I didn't mean for this to happen."

But whether he means the kiss or seeing me again or our entire history, I really don't know.

CHAPTER 4

"THIS IS NICE," *Kiki murmured, as she leaned back against Noah's chest.*

His chin rested on her head, his arms wrapped around her waist. Her own arms were crossed as she held on to him, her thumbs gently brushing his skin, the touch too casual to be any sort of intentional caress—and all the more intimate because of that easy familiarity.

They were standing in front of the floor to ceiling windows that made up the south wall of his Austin condo. Fifteen stories below, the river reflected the pink and purple of the sun that was setting in the west, as if the river was flowing from that melting ball of fire.

"It's beautiful."

"Not as beautiful as you."

She laughed, then met his eyes in the reflection, hers lit with amusement. "That sounds suspiciously like a pick-up line."

"Can it be a line if it's true?"

She shrugged, her attention going back to the river as she sighed with pleasure, her hands tightening on his arms. When she spoke, her voice was soft, and she didn't meet his eyes. "I think the real question is, can it be a line if there's no reason for a pick-up?" She lifted her chin, and when their eyes met in the window this time, he saw a hint of defiance. "After all, you already have me.

Don't you?"

Yes. *He wanted to shout the word, but he couldn't quite force it out past the joy that swelled his chest and filled his heart. Instead, he pressed a kiss to her hair and pulled her tighter against him.*

"Why didn't you surf today?"

For a moment he was confused. Surfing had been almost as much of an obsession as gaming when he was in his early twenties, but he hadn't surfed since—

He shook his head, his mind oddly muddled. And for a moment—only a flash, really—he wasn't looking at the river, but instead at the Pacific, wide and blue and infinite.

He blinked, and the river returned.

"I—I wanted to spend the day with you, of course." He hoped he sounded casual. He felt confused.

"Oh?" There was a tease in her voice. "Why's that?"

He laughed as he spun her in his arms, then found her smiling at him. Her brown eyes seemed to draw him in, and he had to fight the urge to press kisses on each of the freckles that dotted her cheeks. "Happy anniversary, sweetheart. I hope you had a wonderful day."

"You know I did," she said, her eyes so full of love he wanted to drown in them.

"I love you so much." His heart ached with the words. He stroked her soft hair, then wound a teak-colored strand around his finger, relishing the connection.

She cupped his cheek. "Do you think I don't know that? I see it every time you look at me. Every time you touch me."

Small beads of sweat rose at his hairline, and he didn't understand why. But he suddenly felt nervous. Edgy. And he had to swallow to get out the words. "You shouldn't," he whispered, wishing he didn't have to say it. Not understanding why he believed it.

"Shouldn't?" Her brow creased as she shook her head in confusion. "Shouldn't love you?"

He took her hands. He had to make her understand. "All of this," he said emphatically. "None of this matters."

A laugh bubbled out of her, and he saw relief in her eyes. "Of course it doesn't, darling. The only thing that matters is us."

"No." His chest was tight with frustration. Why wasn't she listening? Why couldn't she see?

"Noah?"

"You don't understand." In one quick, horrible movement, he thrust his hands out hard against her chest. He had to do it. How else could he convince her?

Her eyes went wide as she stumbled backward. The glass shattered, and she plummeted out into the void, down and down and down.

He watched her fall, his entire body numb. "You understand now," he whispered, "In the end, I'd only hurt you, too."

HIS OWN GASP of terror woke Noah, and he sat bolt upright in bed, breathing hard, his body as cold as ice.

It was just a dream. He knew that. And he reminded himself of that simple fact again and again as he tried to get back to sleep.

He never managed. Instead, he tossed and turned from three in the morning until five forty-five when the blare of his alarm clock finally gave him permission to quit trying.

Still shaking, he untangled himself from the bed sheets and stumbled into the shower, hoping that the hot water would wash away the remnants of the dream.

It didn't.

On the contrary, the dream infected Noah's entire morning. Over and over, his mind replayed the gut-wrenching image of Kiki endlessly falling, her arms outstretched as she moved inexorably away from him and closer to her horrible, painful fate.

Just a dream. Yes. Right.

But knowing didn't make it any less disturbing, especially since he was both intelligent enough and self-aware enough to understand the origin of the dream. He'd seen Kiki. He'd held her. Touched her.

Most of all, he'd wanted her—with *want* being one of the centuries' most significant understatements—and his subconscious was very firmly reminding him that any path that led to Kiki was a path he had no business following.

But oh how he wanted to.

Even now as he tried and failed to shave without nicking himself, all he could think of was the way she'd felt in his arms. The firmness of her slim body juxtaposed against the softness of her breasts as he held her close, both of them fearing they'd be discovered.

He recalled the scent of rosemary in her hair and the taste of vanilla on her lips. The way his pulse had tripped nervously when he'd closed his mouth over hers, and then the way relief had flooded through him when she responded with equal ardor. At least before the chill that had settled over them both when she'd realized what they were doing.

Hell, even the sting of her hand against his cheek when he'd first encountered her in the alley was a touch to be savored.

She'd always had a quick temper. But like an alchemist's scale, it had been balanced by deep emotion and strong passion. Kiki was a woman who poured her heart into everything, and he knew damn well how much he'd hurt her.

He wanted to make it up to her—but at the same time, he knew that he needed to stay away. He wanted her—dear God, he wanted her—but she had a new life now. One he wasn't part of.

The thought shouldn't bother him, but he couldn't deny that it did.

He'd tasted the past last night—and it had made him crave a future.

But there was just no way.

Oh, sure, he could find her easily enough. Tyree must have her contact information. Or Cam. And even if they wouldn't tell him, Noah wasn't without resources. For years, he'd run tech for a highly effective, covert security operation—which was polite code for *vigilante organization*—and he still had connections and favors to call in.

If he wanted, he could have her address, phone, driving record, and current credit score by the time he walked into his office. And part of him did want. Hell, he wanted so badly it was like a physical ache.

But he couldn't do it.

Couldn't track her down. Couldn't go to her.

Couldn't try to start over.

He wasn't the man she used to know. The Noah she'd fallen in love with had lived in a world of video games and fantasy. A world where he trusted his intellect and creativity to fashion a happy ending both in the games he designed and the life he lived. Kiki had seen only the very beginning of his bitter realization that the world didn't work that way. The world didn't care if you were smart or noble or heroic. The world took what it wanted, and left you to claw your way back from the pain.

The Noah she'd loved had been an optimist.

But the man she'd met last night in an alley had clearer vision. He saw that old Noah for the fool he'd been.

Hell, she didn't even know that Darla and his little girl were dead. That he was alone, and had been for years.

For that matter, he wasn't sure Kiki even knew that he'd had a daughter, only that Darla had been pregnant. Kiki had left Los Angeles before the wedding, and as far as Noah knew, she'd never looked back. She had a new life now, and he wasn't part of it.

He pictured that band leader—Ares?—and wondered if she was seeing him. Were they dating? Married? Did they spend hours bent over the piano, roughing out a song and laughing about ridiculous rhymes?

The thought tasted bitter, and the image of her laughing like that with someone else hurt him more than it should after all these years.

Damn him.

He was being an ass. Much better to let the past stay in the past. To simply hold on tight to his memories. Their time in Los Angeles. Those few stolen moments of bliss last night...

It wasn't enough—it wasn't nearly enough—but he owed her more than the pain of disrupting her life. And God knew, he was damaged goods. In the end, he'd just end up hurting her. Again.

Hadn't his subconscious told him as much in the dream?

As for bumping into her around town...

Well, Austin was a big place, so the odds were slim. And from now on, he'd pay attention to what live music acts were happening at his favorite venues. Not so that he'd know where to go, but so that he'd know where to avoid.

As he finished dressing, he forced himself to think of the day ahead. And by the time he'd walked the four blocks to his office, he'd mostly succeeded in shaking off the dream and the lingering thoughts of Kiki. Today's schedule was too jam-packed—and too important—to let in anything not related to work, and by the time he reached his office and handed his assistant the latte he'd bought for her, his mind was fully on the morning's agenda.

"Thanks," Carina said, taking the drink with a smile that lit up her elfin face.

He'd hired Carina one week after he'd come to Austin with the purpose of turning this floundering tech company into a top competitor in the field of corporate security technology. He'd asked Human Resources to send him a floater to help him get organized, and Carina had swooped in like a combination guardian angel and pit bull, tirelessly organizing him even while ferociously guarding his time by keeping away anyone he didn't truly need to see. After two days, he'd called HR back and told them that she was on his desk permanently.

The coffee ritual started because they were both trying to cut down. The deal was that whenever either of them bought coffee or made a cup in the break room, they had to bring the other one as well. On the whole it was working remarkably well—not only was he paying more attention to how much coffee he drank, but he'd also scored a damn good assistant.

"And you might want to take the toilet paper off before you see Mr. Stark." Her big brown eyes sparkled mischievously.

He rubbed his jaw, knocking off the bit of tissue he'd missed earlier. He'd been so distracted by thoughts of Kiki while shaving that he probably looked like the survivor of a gang fight. Then the full impact of her words hit him. "Damien's here?"

He glanced at the wristwatch he'd inherited from his stepfather five years ago. Before then, he'd always checked the time on his phone. Now, he liked having the reminder. Not only of the only father he'd ever known—a man who'd been unfairly robbed of life at sixty-two when he'd died of an unexpected heart attack—but of the simple fact that time was always too short.

He'd expected Damien about nine-fifteen, just before the first marketing consultant arrived for his pitch at nine-thirty. But according to the analog display, it wasn't yet eight. "He's in my office? Did he say why he came so early?"

She smoothed her short dark hair, a gesture he'd learned was a nervous habit. "All he said was that he was going to wait in your office. I didn't know—I mean, I wasn't sure—"

"It's fine," he assured her, understanding perfectly why even his pit bull would have been too intimidated to suggest Stark wait elsewhere, or to inquire why he'd arrived so early. To put it bluntly, Damien Stark was a force of nature. A former professional tennis player, he'd left the game to launch a multi-billion-dollar international conglomerate with fingers in tech, real estate, entertainment, and so much more. From what Noah had read in the papers and learned for himself, the man had a past even more twisted than Noah's, and an intellect and work ethic that made Noah look like a slacker.

Noah had known Damien socially first through their mutual friend Dallas Sykes, and he'd found the man surprisingly down to earth. But once Noah had come to work for Stark Applied Technology, Noah had witnessed Damien's drive first hand—not to mention how much personal involvement Damien had in all aspects of his empire.

Considering that, he supposed he shouldn't be surprised that Damien had come early. After all, the Austin office was not only a new addition to Stark Applied Technology, having come into existence after Stark bought a dying tech company, but this was also Noah's first time in the hot seat.

Noah shot a last look toward Carina as he headed

toward his office door. "If any of the applicants are early, just show them to the conference room. And here's the notebook," he added, passing her the small leather-bound book that he used to sketch out ideas for the various projects he was pondering at any one time. Ironically low tech considering the work he did, but he enjoyed the feel of a pencil against paper.

Every morning she typed up his notes and scanned his sketches, then returned the notebook after his morning phone calls. Today, he'd get it back after he met with Damien.

And now it was time to enter the ring.

He pulled open the door to his office and stepped inside. Damien was standing by the window, gazing out toward the Capital, and looking completely at home in Noah's office. He turned and smiled as Noah entered. But the smile didn't reach those famous dual-colored eyes.

Until that moment, Noah hadn't realized how on-edge he was. But now he was barraged by all the possible reasons that Damien could have come early—reasons that had been in the back of his mind, and that Damien's stoic expression brought to the surface. A leak of their technology to a competitor. A problem on the assembly line. Litigation about the patents involved.

Hell, it could be anything.

The only thing he didn't question was the viability of the tech itself. Noah didn't consider himself arrogant, but he was both honest and self-critical, and he knew damn well that any potential issue didn't come from his desk.

Still, as the president of Stark Applied Technology Austin, any issue with the project fell on his shoulders. Time to find out just what kind of problem he was facing.

He swept out an arm to indicate the interior of his office. "Welcome to SATA," Noah said, using the abbreviated name that he and his staff used for the business. "What's wrong?"

This time Noah saw amusement in Damien's eyes. "Good morning to you, too."

He took one of the guest chairs, and Noah sat in his usual place behind the desk. Damien Stark might be in the room, but this was Noah's domain, and he felt perfectly at home. "Is there a problem on the line?" he demanded.

The first five hundred units were currently rolling out for limited beta testing. He knew the quality of the Stark plants in Asia was above reproach, but that didn't mean they couldn't hit a snag, and—

"There's no issue with the hardware," Damien said.

Noah nodded, considering Damien's words. On the one hand, he was glad there wasn't a problem on the line. But that left open the question of why Stark had come early. A question that he immediately posed, then followed with, "Or was it just the lure of my sparkling personality?"

"Can you think of a better reason?" Stark retorted.

"Really can't," Noah said, leaning back in his chair. "Although if we have some extra time on our hands, we might consider naming the damn thing." Officially, the tech he'd created was identified as SAT-29X35a. But since that was a mouthful, everyone on the team had begun simply calling it The Project.

"Which is partly what today's pitches are for."

True enough. At nine-thirty the first of ten marketing and product rollout consultants would arrive. Each had submitted a company resume and a brief proposal for the project, and each had been selected from a pool of over fifty potentials. Today, they were coming armed with a specific campaign proposal. Their challenge was to convince Noah and Damien that they had the skill, the contacts, and the vision to both name and fully market The Project.

"To be honest," Damien said, "I came early because we need to talk about a problem with our timeline. And just so you know, I'd hoped to ask you to dinner with Nikki and me tonight just so we could catch up. But unfortunately we have to leave for Milan this evening."

"That is unfortunate," Noah deadpanned.

Damien chuckled. "A problem at one of the Stark properties that I have to take care of personally, but I'll admit that I hope to wrap it up quickly and enjoy a long weekend in Italy with my wife. So I'm afraid dinner's not an option. Are you going to be in LA for Lyle's wrap? He said he invited you."

"Absolutely." Noah had met Lyle Tarpin, one of Hollywood's newest A-listers, not long after he moved to Los Angeles. They'd become good friends. Good enough that Lyle took certain liberties—like setting up Noah on blind dates with pretty lawyers. "It's on a Thursday, so I'll probably fly in that morning."

"Good. We can catch up more then."

"Looking forward to it. But what about the time-line?"

"It's been slashed." Noah heard the edge in Damien's voice.

"For the rollout?" Noah did some mental math, and the answer he came up with was *What the hell?*

They'd already planned on a fast and hard campaign. He wasn't sure they could move any faster or any harder, and he told Damien as much.

"I didn't get where I am today by being the second man to any party," Damien said. "Trust me when I say that we're going to have competition. And that's fine. Competition doesn't scare me. But I want us to be the first through the door."

Noah sifted through everything Damien was suggesting. "Someone leaked my design?"

"Not as far as I can tell. But The Project is a natural progression of your listening device that I licensed, and that's been commercially available for couple of years now."

"But only to governments, military, and contractors." Even as he said it, Noah knew his words were nonsense. Damien was right.

The listening device functioned like any bug that might be planted by the police or a private security team. But unlike those devices—which required breaching the premises—Noah's tech accessed the entirety of a building through the building's electrical system, then filtered all the internal chatter into an infinite number of channels that could either be monitored live or with keywords input into an AI-operated review system. So far, the device was most useful to off-book, covert security teams, but some law enforcement agencies were looking into using it upon receipt of a warrant.

Noah had invented the device while he was working at Deliverance, the covert organization founded by billionaire Dallas Sykes, which specialized in locating and rescuing kidnap victims. Because the existence of Deliverance was known only to a key few, Dallas didn't use his own corporate connections to manufacture Noah's device. But they'd needed it, and fast, and so Damien Stark had been pulled into the secret. Stark had licensed the tech for Stark Applied Technology—giving Noah a hefty royalty that produced an income in excess of anything he'd ever imagined—and provided Deliverance with the original prototypes and the final tech.

After a while, Stark recruited Noah as well, which was easy enough to do. Noah believed in the work Deliverance did, but he'd needed to heal, and to do that, he'd needed to escape the daily reminder of his wife and daughter.

He'd originally come to work for SAT in Los Angeles, and his focus had been on both new tech and the expansion of the listening device to the limits of the design. The Project piggybacked off the original tech, utilizing significant AI technology to construct a full building control and monitoring system. And because of the nature of the technology, it could be adapted for everything from covert military use on the one end to suburban home operation on the other.

From the get-go, Stark had seen the potential and had provided Noah with whatever development resources he'd needed. Noah had worked round the clock, not because he was in a race with a competitor, but because the work itself pushed him on.

Noah frowned, thinking about all the hours he'd put in. Hours that someone else with skill and vision might make obsolete.

"Who?" he demanded.

"It's still a rumor, but it's a solid one," Damien said. "My intelligence indicates that an Israeli-based company with military connections is close to rolling out their own prototype of a remarkably similar product. If it's earmarked only for the military, then all that does is remove a significant chunk of our potential customer base."

Noah nodded. "But the odds are that they'll develop a private, retail version, too."

"Which means the clock is ticking," Damien said.

Noah sighed, the possibility of all his work being swept away was almost too horrible to contemplate. He drew in a breath and let it out slowly. "I guess we better hope at least one of these consultants knows what they're doing."

That, however, was a hope that died a slow and painful death.

The morning's first two applicants were probably fine at their jobs, but neither brought anything new or innovative to the table, despite repeatedly saying that they were up to the task and the faster rollout wouldn't be a problem.

The third assured them that the compressed timeline wouldn't be a problem, then spent the rest of the meeting justifying his increased fee without any explanation of how his plan would change to fit the new parameters.

By the time the sixth—another dud—left, Noah was starting to think he ought to chuck it all and go back to writing video games. At the very least, he was confident all the applicants would know how to market that.

"We haven't seen one with an innovative approach," Noah said.

Damien nodded in agreement. In the meetings, he looked equally fresh for all the applicants. But now, as they waited for contestant number seven, he pinched the bridge of his nose and looked as tired as Noah felt. "It's not just innovation we need. The product itself is innovative. We need a company with ideas that are fresh enough to match our product."

That morning, Noah would have agreed. Now, he feared that Damien was asking too much.

To keep Damien from seeing his frustration, Noah focused on the resume submitted by the next applicant, Kimberly Porter, the owner of Crown Consulting. She'd worked on a variety of rollouts, everything from the high-visibility, nationwide retail products all the way through to announcements of new drilling techniques that were advertised only within the trade itself.

More than that, her resume suggested a certain finesse. Whether or not she had the vision for this project ... well, Noah could only hope. She was the seventh of ten, and if one of these last four didn't work out, they'd end up even further behind the curve.

The intercom buzzed. "Ms. Porter is here," Carina said as Damien and Noah both stood in greeting. "I'll show her in."

A moment passed before Carina tapped lightly on the door. It opened as Noah glanced down at the resume on the table and took a second to say a silent prayer that Kimberly Porter was different from all the rest.

Then he looked up, saw her, and felt the room tilt absurdly to the left.

He grabbed the edge of the table to steady himself, barely even noticing that her astonished expression mirrored exactly how he felt.

She was different, all right.

She was Kiki.

CHAPTER 5

"NOAH?"

His name slips past my lips before I can help myself, and I stumble backward, as if an invisible hand has reached out and shoved hard against my chest. For a second, the thought skitters through my mind that I could spin around and bolt down the hallway to the elevator.

Of course, we're on the twenty-second floor, so the odds are good that Noah would reach me before the elevator came to deliver me to safety.

Assuming he came after me at all.

Ugh.

I'm trapped in a walking, talking, waking nightmare. The kind where the world doesn't make sense, where the ground shifts beneath you, and where the buildings rearrange themselves every time you turn around.

"Have you two worked together before?" The voice comes from the man sitting across the table from Noah. He has raven-black hair, a chiseled jaw, and a demeanor that demands both attention and respect.

I've never met him before, but I know he's Damien Stark. I did my research on the company, after all. But even if I hadn't, I would have recognized the man. How could I not? Stark's a constant fixture in the news for both his work and his personal life.

Which rather neatly illustrates how much seeing Noah has flustered me. Because until Stark spoke, I hadn't even noticed he was in the room.

Apparently, I need to get a grip, but it's not every day I see ghosts. And yet this week, I'm haunted by the ghost of relationships past.

I clear my throat and pump up the volume on my game-ready smile. "We did," I say. "Back in Los Angeles." I step briskly into the room and position myself at the head of the conference table, so I'm looking down it toward the two men. "I have to apologize. I don't usually stand in doorways and gape. I was just surprised."

"Ms. Porter did the music for a video game I designed." He meets my eyes, and I look away. I'm too overwhelmed by the force of the memories that crash over me. Our time in LA. And, damn me, that kiss last night.

"But that was a lifetime ago," Noah finishes, his voice steady and cool. And even though he's taking my lead by mentioning only our professional collaboration, I can't help the twinge of pain that comes from his easy dismissal of everything that was between us.

Good grief, I'm a mess.

I clutch tight to my leather portfolio, willing it to pull me back into professional mode. "I had no idea I'd see you here today," I say in an even tone without any note of accusation at all. But, seriously. The guy took the time to kiss me last night. Couldn't he have taken an extra two seconds and warned me?

I shift my attention back to Mr. Stark. "I did my research on the company after receiving the RFP, but I somehow missed Mr. Carter's involvement."

"That's on me," Stark says. "We issued the original Request for Proposal through the main office in Los Angeles. At the time, the Austin office was still in transition."

"I'm sorry I didn't let you know," Noah adds, reminding me of the way he always seemed to be able to read my mind. "But I had no idea you were Kimberly Porter."

"Oh. Of course." I feel like a fool. I've spent years intentionally not searching out information about Noah. At first, it was hard to force myself not to look. He'd hurt me, and like most wounded people, I'd wanted to pick at the scab even while I was trying to heal.

But I'd gathered my strength and resisted the urge. Fortunately, social media wasn't as vibrant back then. I was on MySpace with Pink Chameleon, but that was about it.

Later, of course, it would have been easier to track him down. But by then, the scab had turned to a scar, and my resolve was stronger. So I'd walked into this room without any expectation at all that he would be here.

And yet, despite all that, some part of me had believed that even while I was avoiding him, he was keeping an eye on me. Watching the way my music career spiraled down. Making a note of the fact that I'd finally given up on ever writing a song again and had enrolled at UT to pursue an MBA. Getting married to Owen.

It's humbling to realize he didn't know any of that. To be faced so blatantly with the simple truth that we were young, that we'd shared an intense passion, and that we've both moved on.

Or we had until we met in a dark alley, and all that heat and lust and longing came rushing back.

Once again, I turn my attention to Mr. Stark. "When we knew each other, I was Kimberly King," I explain. "I started using Porter when I got married. But everyone still calls me Kiki."

I don't look at Noah. And I definitely don't mention that I'm divorced. Under the circumstances, I think I'll hold that little factoid close to the vest.

Under the circumstances.

What exactly does that mean?

The circumstances are that I've prepped the shit out of this assignment. That I want this job, and that I need it desperately.

But that's not all. Unfortunately, the circumstances also include the memory of last night's kiss, and the way I melted in his arms. I may have been the one to push him away, but that didn't stop the flood of wildly erotic images invading my dreams last night.

Which means that if I want to toss up the specter of my former husband as a barrier between me and future temptation, I think I'm entirely justified. Noah may not be loyal to his spouse, but my loyalty to the institution of marriage and the small fraud I'm perpetrating runs deep.

Too bad I'm not wearing a wedding ring to complete

the illusion. Then again, Noah's not wearing one either. But some men don't. Some women, too. Maybe I'm a woman who doesn't want to follow convention either. Maybe I—

Stop it.

I'm not someone who shakes easily, and the fact that I'm mentally all over the place on such an important day is frustrating as hell. Yes, this is a nightmare situation, but I'm still standing, which means I've aced the hardest part. Now I need to kick the past to the curb, and all non-business thoughts of Noah along with it.

Determined to get back on track, I give myself a firm mental yank, then flash a confident, easy smile at both men. It's time to pull myself together, act like a professional, and win this assignment.

The good news is that I genuinely love my job. The even better news is that I've been preparing like a maniac for this presentation, because I have too much riding on this opportunity. Land this project, and my life will be very firmly on the right track after having been derailed for so many years.

Blow it, and I'm going to have to make some really hard decisions.

A lot of pressure, sure. But I do well under pressure, and by the time I've set up my laptop and am walking both men through the plan overview, the past with Noah has faded away. All that matters now is convincing a potential client that I'm the best for the job. And since this was an open RFP, I know who my competition is. And, dammit, I really am the best.

As I move through the various elements of my proposal, I can see by Noah and Stark's faces that they know it, too.

"I'm impressed," Noah says when I finally step back from my computer and ask if they have any questions. His words are simple, but they mean a lot. I know how important quality is to him, and I also know he pushes himself as hard as his team. He's not a man who gives an A for effort. If he says he's impressed, he means it.

"You've managed to present a cohesive plan that integrates all of our potential markets, and at the same time treats each market and its relationship to the product distinctly. There's overlap, but only minimal."

Like a schoolgirl, I blush with pleasure.

Stark nods agreement. "It's a surgical strike plan. If it's executed properly, the results will likely exceed your projections."

"I was being conservative," I admit, imagining the feel of the pen in my hand as I sign my name to the consulting contract.

"Nothing wrong with that," Stark says. "But the big question is the *if*." His words bring me down to earth.

"If I can pull it off?" I keep my tone both casual and confident. "I hope my proposal and my resume illustrate my skill in reaching—and exceeding—all projections and project milestones."

"Confidence is a valuable tool," Noah says. "And your skill is proven by your resume and what you showed us here today. But we're working under a tighter timeline now."

I raise a brow, then look between both men.

"There are rumors we'll lose our competitive edge if

we don't jump on this quickly," Noah says, then passes me a print-out with the new, tighter schedule.

"Oh." I feel a twinge of irritation that neither man told me that from the get-go. But that's quickly replaced by the realization that this is a test. Am I innovative and flexible? Damn right I am.

I turn my laptop back on and step to the white board where my summary slide is being projected. I snatch up a marker, and proceed to edit my plan right in front of them, talking through each element and how I would revise it to meet the tighter deadlines. "It will be a challenge," I say. "Then again, you both already knew that." I point to my notations. "But it's doable."

"It is," Noah says with a nod. "If you have the staff to make it happen."

He's right, of course. And the truth is, I don't. My operation is small, with only three of us working full-time. Me, of course. Maia, who's been my right-hand for years, and who I've just asked to come on board as my partner. And our office manager.

My practice is to staff up for each project, using trusted freelancers I've worked with before. I've already put five on notice. But getting a larger team together for this new timeframe will be tricky.

Since bullshitting won't get me anywhere, I tell Noah and Stark exactly that, and am rewarded by the flicker of both surprise and respect in their eyes.

"Are you saying that you're withdrawing your pro-posal?" Noah focuses on my face as he asks the question. And I can't tell if his expression holds relief or disappointment.

"Not at all," I say, my mind churning as I struggle to salvage this problem. "I'm proposing that my team utilize Stark employees."

Sometimes, I love my subconscious. I hadn't planned that approach, but it makes the most sense. It's already my practice on large jobs to have my team move into a conference room on-site so that we have easy access to the company's support staff. All I'm proposing now is that we go even further.

Even though Stark International and all its subsidiaries have excellent in-house marketing, I'm not surprised they're using an outside contractor for a roll-out such as this—a man like Stark knows the value of specialization. But at the same time, I'm sure there are oodles of Stark employees across the globe who are more than capable of providing support for a rollout of this nature.

I can practically see my thought process reflected on Mr. Stark's face—and the fact that he doesn't dismiss the idea outright gives me hope.

As for Noah, I'm almost afraid to look at him. Because if he and Stark accept this revised proposal, then I'll be moving in. This very conference room may be command central, and I'll be working intimately with him and the team every single day.

The thought gives me pause, but only for a moment, then I'm firmly back on the giddy train.

The intercom buzzes, which I recognize as a signal from the assistant who walked me in that my time is up. They still have more candidates to interview, but I know the guys who are about to pitch, and they're not pressure players. Which means that unless Stark and Noah saw something seriously impressive before I walked through the door, I'm confident this job is mine.

"Ms. Porter," Stark says, rising to shake my hand, "it's been a pleasure."

"Good seeing you again," Noah says. His voice reflects only corporate politeness. But his handshake is firm, and though I don't want it to, his touch sends my body humming.

"You too," I say, trying to tug my hand free without being obvious.

"We'll be in touch," he adds, as the dark-haired assistant leads me out the door and back to the elevator. I walk calmly, but it's not easy. What I want to do is skip.

And once I'm alone on the elevator, I do exactly that.

Because I nailed it. This job is mine.

Am I a marketing goddess or what?

"I'M AN IDIOT, aren't I?"

It's barely eight in the morning, and I'm sitting morosely at my breakfast bar watching Ares pour green sludge from my Vitamix into a tumbler.

"Pretty much," he says, then shoves the drink in front of me. Here," he says. "You're thin as a rail."

"Well, no wonder, if this is the kind of stuff you're feeding me. There's not an ounce of chocolate in here, much less ice cream."

He smirks, and I smile sweetly back. But I also do as he asks and take a sip of the nasty thing. These last few months, all my attention has gone to writing songs and working up the Stark proposal. Mundane things like eating and having a life have fallen by the wayside.

The upside is that I can probably market my eating plan and make a mint. The downside is that I would be vilified across the globe. A diet of coffee and rice is hardly a nutritious choice.

"That was gross," I say honestly, after I've choked the kale flavored mouthful down. But I am hungry, and it is healthy. "I'm pretty sure you're the devil," I say, then take another sip.

"No, I'm just her cousin."

That makes me laugh, which leads to me almost snorting green smoothie through my nose. But it's worth it for the mental picture of Celia with little red devil horns.

My best friend and former band mate is both organized and bossy, which makes her annoying, though not truly evil. But that doesn't mean I'll forego teasing her, even *in absentia*.

Ares takes a sip of his own smoothie and swallows it without any signs of gagging or disgust. "Okay, tell me. Why are you an idiot? Other than all the reasons I'm familiar with, I mean."

"Be nice to me," I say. "Free living space, remember?"

Since Seven Percent is heading out on tour next week, he rented out his cute little Central Austin house for the next five months. But the band doesn't hit the road until Monday. Which means he's camping in my spare bedroom until then.

"Not free," he says. "Barter." He lifts the smoothie. "I'm feeding you."

I snort. "There's one reason I'm an idiot. Agreeing to put up with you for a weekend."

He flashes the same wide grin that has girls scrambling up on stage when he's performing. "Bite your tongue."

"Did that once," I say. "Left a bad taste."

He laughs. "Bitch."

"Asshole."

"But you love me," he says, and he's right. I do. I just don't *love* him. We did the dating thing for about a week, after doing the casual sex thing when I was still morose about my failed marriage and leaving Owen. Or, more specifically, when I thought I should be morose.

There were never relationship sparks with Ares, though, much to Celia's disappointment. But we have friendship sparks in spades.

"You're avoiding the question," Ares says. "Why are you an idiot this time?"

I leave the smoothie on the bar and move to my sofa, then stretch out, getting comfy. I'm wearing my sushi pattern pajama bottoms paired with a *Texas Strong* tanktop. Ares joins me, and I lift my feet only long enough to let him sit so that I can put them in his lap. "The job, of course."

His brow furrows. "I thought it was the perfect gig. Wasn't that what you said when you first got the RFP? In fact, I seem to remember you waving the paper, dancing around this very room, and singing about it being a really big gig. You were off key, by the way."

"The hell I was, and the job is perfect. Or it was. Now I'm afraid I'm going to get it."

"With the way your mind works, it's a wonder you don't go through life in a perpetual state of vertigo."

I smirk. "It's just ... *Noah*."

"Are you still in love with him?"

The question shocks me. It's so simple. So basic. And so very unexpected that I have to take a few moments to think about it. "No," I finally say. "How could I be after all this time? I mean, we don't even know each other anymore. Not really."

"Then what's the problem?"

I exhale, because apparently *I'm* the problem. "Because I *am* still in love with the Noah who lives in my head. The one who broke my heart. I'm in love with his memory, with the dreams that I had to let go. And I know it's going to hurt like hell to be working side by side with him."

He presses his hand lightly against my ankle, his storm-gray eyes on mine as he nods thoughtfully. "I get that. And it may not be an issue. He may be thinking the exact same thing. It may be bothering him so much that he doesn't offer you the position."

I bolt up, fueled by irritation. "Whoa," I say. "That would be totally unfair. I kicked ass on that proposal. He can't just take me out of the running. He needs to get over it."

"You think it's that easy?"

"Of course not, but—oh." I flop back against my pillow, ceding his victory. "I guess I should be able to get over it, too, huh?"

"It's worth trying to, isn't it? I know Celia will have your head on a platter if you back out of the album. And she'll have mine for not convincing you."

He's right, of course. For the last few months, Celia and I have been working toward reviving Pink Chameleon. And the more we've accomplished, the more excited I've become.

I do love my work, but I miss writing and performing. But the nature of my business is such that I can handpick my projects, and that's what I did with the Stark proposal. Get this job—get this paycheck—and I'll have enough money to live for a year in LA while Celia and I compile a new body of work, and then rehearse, record, and possibly even hit the road for a short tour depending on the reaction to the singles we'll release.

And now that the Stark money stays the same but the time period is truncated, it's an even better deal for me. Get in, get out, get financed.

The beautiful thing is that I don't even have to walk away from Crown Consulting. With Maia coming on as my partner, she can run the shop while I'm gone, and I'll chime in as needed from Los Angeles or the road.

In other words, the Stark job would give me the chance to make it in the career that Noah stole from me ... and also in the one he pushed me toward. Because before he broke my heart and killed my muse, he'd been my biggest fan and my most vocal cheerleader.

But without the income from this job, I can't afford to take time off. I can still plan the Pink Chameleon revival, but it will take longer and be messier.

If the dice roll that way, then I'll deal with it. But if I

actively screw it all up by walking away from the Stark job…

Well, Ares is right. Celia will go all *Game of Thrones* on me, and I'll be her very best decapitated friend.

"Of course, if you don't get the job—or you decide you don't want the job—my offer still stands."

I roll my eyes. Ares has repeatedly asked me to go on tour with Seven Percent. Historically, they've been a fully male group, though I wouldn't call them a boy band any more than The Police or The Rolling Stones were boy bands back in the day. But now he wants a female lead singer in the mix. One who, like me, can also play guitar when vocals aren't an issue.

I won't deny that I'm tempted, but Pink Chameleon is my baby. And if there's a chance of reviving it, that's a chance I'm taking.

A terrifying chance, sure. But I'm finally ready for it. At least, I think I am. And this job will help me get there.

I look up at Ares, and he grins, obviously seeing my conclusion on my face.

"It's going to be crazy working with Noah," I say.

"You're both adults. It'll be fine."

Sure. Right. I bob my head as I consider. "Maybe," I admit. "And maybe it'll even be nice to get to know him again. I mean, I've always admired his work ethic. I'll probably learn a lot."

"When will you hear?"

I automatically glance toward the kitchen and the clock that flashes on the microwave, though I don't know why. Neither Noah nor Stark gave a specific time. "They said they'd make notifications today," I tell Ares.

"I'm not sure when."

"Then let's go out. Get your mind off it. It's a gorgeous day. Want to take the bikes out?" I live in South Austin near the Ladybird Wildflower Center and the Austin Veloway.

I consider that, decide it's a damn good plan, and tell him so. "Give me ten to change."

I'm back in leggings and one of my favorite sport tanks with a built-in bra. It's November, and the weather is brisk. But it's also Austin, which means that brisk is pretty tame. I'll grab a jacket on my way out the door, but I'll probably end up tying it around my waist when I get warm on the bike.

Ares is already changed into biking shorts—which reminds me why I slept with him that one and only time—and a Seven Percent T-shirt. "Ready?" He passes me my water bottle as we head to the door.

"Let's hit Magnolia for lunch on the way home," I say as I reach my door. I'm looking at him as I pull it open, and so I'm completely unprepared when I turn back to the doorway and see Noah standing right there, his hand lifted to knock.

"Oh! Noah!"

Behind me, Ares moves over, obviously wanting to get a view of who's in the door. "Right," he says. "I'll be in the bedroom."

And then the bastard abandons me.

"Sorry about showing up unannounced," Noah says. "I should have called." He lifts his hand higher, and I'm certain he's about to run his fingers through his hair. But he checks himself and puts his hand in his pocket. From the untidy state of his hair, I'm thinking that this is the first time this morning that he's resisted the urge.

"It's okay," I say, though I'm not sure it is. I'd been relaxed and confident only a few minutes before. Now I feel like a teenager talking with a crush.

Damn me.

I flash a professional smile. "What's up?"

It's a perfunctory question. He's here because of the job, of course. Because I got it, and he wants to tell me in person so that we can talk off-premises about working around any lingering awkwardness. And since I'm all for that, I flash an easy, welcoming smile. "You have news?"

"I do." He swallows, and I notice the way his eyes drift over me. I cross my arms, suddenly realizing how skin-tight my outfit is.

Noah clears his throat. "Um, right. Well, I thought it would be best to tell you in person."

I nod, and he draws a breath.

He's going to offer, and I'm going to accept, and then I'm going to celebrate by ordering gingerbread pancakes with my migas at Magnolia, and Ares can just kiss my not-so-healthy ass.

I'm about to usher Noah in so that all of that doesn't have to happen on my porch, but he speaks before I can step out of the way.

"I'm sorry, Kiki," he says, as I try to process those words. "We're going with someone else."

CHAPTER 6

A S FAR AS Noah was concerned, his miserable fucking morning turned into a miserable fucking afternoon. And, unfortunately, that status didn't show any signs of improving now that the end of the workday was drawing near.

Then again, why would it? It's not as if he was going to do anything for the rest of the night except remember Kiki's horrified expression as he'd tossed a hand grenade through her front door.

All day, he'd been replaying that scene in his head. Over and over and over again.

Him, trying to be calm and rational as he gave her the bad news.

Her, going completely pale before lurching forward and slamming the door so hard that it almost broke his nose. Now, he had an abraded wrist and a sore ankle from leaping backward, then scraping his arm as he blindly reached out to catch himself. He'd missed, and he'd winced with pain as he stumbled off the low, stone step that served as a front stoop.

Not his most graceful moment. And his wrist hurt like a mother, but he supposed he deserved it. He should never have gone in person. He should have called her like he'd called the other candidates.

But, damn him, he'd wanted to see her again. Because this time, he knew, would be the last time.

Fuck it. With a violent shove, he pushed back from his desk and stood up. He looked out the window and imagined that he could find her out there. Maybe she was right below him, setting up a microphone at some bar on Sixth Street for a performance later tonight. Maybe she was still in her house, out of view, but tucked away beyond the spread of green on the far side of the river.

Wherever she was, he knew that right now she hated him. Why shouldn't she? God knew he hated himself.

With another violent curse, he turned back to his desk, then picked up the manila folder with the resumes of the two consultants he was still considering. He and Stark had selected the final three candidates, but then Damien had left, telling Noah that, as the front man, he needed to pick his own team.

Damien was right, of course. And Noah had made the first move by eliminating Kiki. As for the rest, it shouldn't be this difficult. Noah should have made his decision by now and then texted Damien to give him the final word, but he kept vacillating. It wasn't a question of selecting the best candidate. It was a question of which was the better of two inferior candidates.

The best was Kiki, hands down.

But that was a determination based on her skill set and proposed plan, and that was only one factor in a much larger equation. An equation that included almost a decade of pain, hurt feelings, and inevitable distractions. An equation that had the two of them working together practically round-the-clock for three months.

Frustrated, he shoved the folders into the canvas and leather messenger bag he used instead of a briefcase. It was only five, and he never left the office this early, but he was feeling trapped. Maybe the walk home would clear his head and magically hand him a decision.

He punched the intercom on his desk. "Carina, I'm heading out. Tell reception they can transfer calls to my cell until seven."

"Of course. But—"

"After that, I'm shutting down." Still distracted, he released the button and headed for the door.

"Mr. Carter." Her voice rang out from the intercom speaker, and he frowned. He was halfway to the door, and she was right outside his office at her desk. Easier to just step into the waiting area. "What is—"

The question died on his lips. *It* was Kiki. Standing right next to Carina's desk, her posture stiff and formal as her brown eyes looked accusingly at him.

"Ms. Porter just arrived," Carina said, shooting him a sympathetic glance. "But since you're on your way out, perhaps I should schedule an appointment for next week?"

"Oh, hell no," Kiki said, the formal stance sloughing off to reveal a woman he remembered only too well. They hadn't fought much, but when they did, it was loud and raucous, and always followed by intense make-up sex.

Somehow, he had a feeling that wasn't the way today's encounter was going to wrap up.

"I want an explanation, Noah."

"Mr. Carter?" Carina's eyes were wide and her hands flat on the desk, as if she was about to lever herself up and leap into the line of fire.

"Everything's fine," he said, deciding right then to give Carina a raise. It had missed the mark, but he appreciated that she'd thrown herself up as a wall between him and the angry, spurned candidate.

He also wondered if she'd still be defending him if she knew the whole story. If she knew that Kiki presented the best proposal by far, but that he was hesitant to give her the job because there might be friction.

Might be?

He glanced at Kiki and sighed. He'd tried to avoid friction, and yet friction had marched right into his waiting room. "We need to talk."

"Gee, you think?" She started to walk toward his office.

"No, this way." He took her elbow, then turned her around, the touch too damn familiar.

He yanked his hand away and caught Carina's expression in the process. Confusion, but with a tiny spark that might be understanding.

He turned his attention back to Kiki. One woman irritated with him was all he could handle at the moment. "I'm leaving. If you want to talk, we can do it on the move." Not exactly a stunning example of wresting back control of the situation, but at least she didn't argue.

Two minutes later—in the cattle car of an elevator—he was regretting his decision. His office would have been easier.

Maybe Noah never left this early, but it seemed everyone else in the building did. The car was jam-packed. It hadn't been when they'd first stepped on. Just six people plus him and Kiki. He'd moved to the back, and she'd stood beside him.

By the time the elevator had made three more stops, she was directly in front of him, and the car was so crowded that he was flat against the back wall and she was so close that he felt the brush of her against his slacks.

There was a time when he would have hooked his arm around her waist and pulled her against him, his lips in her hair, her scent enveloping him, and his cock hard against her backside as they rode down together, both of them fantasizing about what they'd do if they only had the elevator to themselves.

"We're here," he said as the elevator glided to a stop at the lobby. The man standing in front of her stepped forward, and she practically leaped into the space he vacated. Coincidence? Or had her thoughts been traveling in a similar direction to his, and she'd rushed to get clear?

"Do you want a coffee?" he asked as they stepped outside and into the brisk November air, raising the possibility both because he wanted something to say and because he could really use the caffeine jolt.

"What the *hell* is wrong with you?" she demanded.

"Caffeine deprivation, primarily," he said as he stepped into the intersection, crossing Congress Avenue with the flood of downtown employees escaping their offices for home. He watched them enviously. There was a time when he'd wanted nothing but to be at her side. Now he just wanted to get to his condo, take two ibuprofens, and hope that tomorrow was a damn sight better than today.

"Oh, no," she said, keeping pace with him. "I waited for you to drag me away from your starry-eyed protégé, but enough is enough."

He battled a smile. "You mean Carina?"

"She looks loyal. Wouldn't want her to realize that her boss is a conniving prick who'll do anything to protect his own ass."

Considering Noah himself hadn't decided if not hiring her was smart or idiotic, he'd expected her to challenge his decision. This, however, was nuts.

"Protecting myself? Just because I want what's best for the project?"

"Oh, that's rich."

He shook his head, which only exacerbated his growing headache. He pointed to the nearby Starbucks, as he continued that direction. "Coffee, then home. That's my current itinerary, and if you want me to alter it, then you need to give me a reason other than bullshit. You're the one who barged into my office because she's a sore loser."

Shit. Had he really said that? What was he, stuck in middle school and yanking the ponytail of the cute girl who ignored him?

"Me? I'm not the one who settled for second best because I can't deal with the reality of my own personal life."

He stopped and gaped at her. "I can't deal? *I* can't

deal? You're the one nervous about working with me."

Her eyes went wide. "Excuse me?"

"Oh, come on," he said, taking a step closer. "Don't pretend to misunderstand."

"You're imagining things."

"Am I?" He took another step, so that he was right in front of her. She could back up more—they were at least eighteen inches from the building's facade—but she held her ground. He stopped only inches from her. Close enough that he could smell her shampoo and see the pale ghosts of the freckles she'd tried to hide under her makeup. Once upon a time, he'd spent hours in bed kissing each and every one of those freckles. Now, he didn't even have the right to touch them.

He wanted to, though.

The realization slammed against him with visceral, powerful intensity. Their kiss on Wednesday had been a succulent appetizer. Now, he wanted the full course. They both did—he was certain of it.

And that, of course, was the problem.

"I think you need to get over yourself," she said. But she was looking at his face, and her words betrayed her, coming a second too late and just a little too breathy.

"Don't tell me you haven't thought about that kiss, too." He reached out and brushed his thumb over her lower lip. But the caress was cut short when she jerked her chin with a sharp, "Don't."

"You've played it over and over in your mind," he said, and saw confirmation in the guarded expression on her face. "And you were worried that we couldn't work together. That this thing between us would get in the way." He met her eyes. "Weren't you?"

She swallowed, her freckles standing out against the pink of her rising blush. She started moving again, sliding back into the flow of pedestrian traffic. "There's no 'thing' between us."

"The hell there isn't." Her legs were shorter than his, but he still had to work to keep pace. "There always has been. It was there the day we met. It was in the alley that night. It's between us right now. Lie about your marriage if you want to, but don't lie about that."

"What?" The word lashed out like a whip. "Lie about my marriage?"

"Don't pretend you don't know what I mean," he countered. He wasn't proud of himself, but from the moment she'd said she was married, he'd needed to know to whom. He wanted to know what the man did. How long they'd been together. If he was worthy of having Kiki by his side.

He still had access to the Deliverance databases, and even though he'd battled back the urge to check up on her for years, last night he'd succumbed. Now he knew she'd married Owen Porter, a professor at the University of Texas, six years ago. And he knew they'd divorced eighteen months after they'd exchanged vows.

"You tossed your marriage up like a shield," he continued. "Problem is, you're not married anymore."

"Trust me," she said, with a tone of self-mockery. "That's *really* not a problem."

He fought the smile that rose with the knowledge that she didn't regret her divorce. "Maybe, but you still put your marriage between us, just like building a wall."

She paused long enough to look him up and down and shake her head. "You're delusional." She started walking again, not waiting for his response. "I mentioned my married name, which just so happens to be the name I use now. There was no hidden meaning."

"Bullshit. You wanted to distance yourself. You were nervous about working together."

She was picking up speed, but he was done with chasing her. He reached out and grabbed her hand, tugging her to a stop. They'd passed the Starbucks long ago, and were now at Third Street. A right turn and another block, and they'd be at his condo.

"Come on, Kiki, admit it. You wouldn't have even responded to the RFP if you'd known it was me you were pitching to."

For a moment, she simply stood there, her hand in his, her expression entirely unreadable. Then she sighed, her shoulders dipping as if in surrender. "Probably not," she admitted. "But I didn't know, and I did go, and when I saw you, I didn't pull myself out of the running. And we both know that my pitch was the best, don't we?"

He stayed silent, and she rolled her eyes. "You think I don't know my competition's strengths and weaknesses?"

"Fine," he said. "You put up a rock solid proposal, but even while you were standing there pitching, you knew it would be hard to work together. And you know what? You were right." He dragged his fingers through his hair. "Christ, Kiki, do you think I don't know how much I hurt you? How much I owe you?"

Her brow furrowed as her expression turned wary.

"I do," he continued. "I owe you more than I can ever pay, but at the very least I owe you the courtesy of not dragging you in and disrupting your life all over again."

For a flicker of a moment, her features softened. But even as he watched, he saw the tension return. "I can't believe you." With an exasperated shake of her head, she started walking again. "You're laying all this at my feet? What about you?" she added as he fell into step beside her.

"Maybe you're feeling a little guilty for that kiss?" she continued. "Have you told Darcy or Daisy or whatever the fuck wifey's name is that you locked lips with your old girlfriend in a dark alley? Because I'm thinking you haven't. And I'm thinking she won't be happy when she learns it's your ex-girlfriend who's working late nights with you on this rollout. Better to avoid that problem entirely and just go with the candidate behind door number two."

He drew a slow breath, as guilt, regret, and longing twisted together to form a thick, tight knot in his stomach. After a moment, he said, "I haven't been married to Darla for a very long time."

"Oh." The word was soft and simple, and as far as he could tell, entirely devoid of emotion. She stopped walking and repeated. "Oh."

He considered explaining. Telling her the whole horrible story. But now wasn't the time. Maybe there never would be a time. Instead he said, "All I was trying to do was make things easier on you."

She winced a little, as if his words hurt her. "Maybe,"

she finally said, her voice no longer bitter, but gentle. "But that's not your call to make. If it hurt *you* to see me, then maybe that's fair. But you're not shutting me out because *you're* going to be uncomfortable, but because you think I am."

She was only half right, but he kept that to himself. "Well, aren't you?" he asked instead. "Uncomfortable, I mean."

"Of course." She squared her shoulders as she gathered courage, the posture and its meaning so achingly familiar even after all these years. "You said there was a thing between us, and you're right. Wednesday night in your arms was horrible and wonderful. And later that night—oh, my God, the dreams."

He couldn't fight back his smile. "Oh, really? Care to elaborate?"

She smirked, her expression suggesting that she was amazed they'd drifted into such dangerous conversational waters. To her credit, she didn't backpedal.

"I didn't expect to see you again," she continued. "And I won't deny the shock when I walked into that conference room. And I won't lie about how hard it is to stand here with you. To be this close to you and know that we aren't what we used to be. Is the desire still there? Hell, yes. And maybe it would be better if we hadn't shared that stupid kiss. It was like flipping a switch, and bringing something dormant roaring back to life."

"Kiki—"

"No. Let me finish. It wasn't closure, but it also wasn't a beginning. It just *was*." She flashed a self-deprecating grin. "This may come as a shock to you, but I've passed the thirty marker. I've got a house. I've got a car. I have a brokerage account and a cleaning lady who comes every two weeks. I even own a life insurance policy.

"In other words, I've been taking care of myself for a long time now, and I don't need you stepping in to unilaterally decide what's best and then yanking the things I want out from under me. I've been there with you, Noah. And we have most definitely done that. And I'm not going down that road quietly again."

She'd switched from the present to the past, and he knew it. But he wasn't willing to talk about their time in Los Angeles, or Darla, or any of it. Not yet.

The only thing on the table right now was this job. That, and the desire that sparked and crackled between them like a downed power line that they were both trying desperately to avoid.

"I didn't yank it away," he said. "I made a decision. That's my job."

"Your job is to decide on the basis of my work. Not because you're trying to soothe my poor little broken heart. In case you missed the key point on my resume, I'm a professional."

"You're right."

Her brows rose. "I am?"

He nodded. She'd worn him down, but maybe he always knew that she would. After all, he hadn't offered the job to anyone else yet, either.

It would be okay. They'd worked together before, hadn't they? They could do it again. So what if he wanted to touch her? What did it matter if he wanted to feel her against him again? To discover if the memory of her body pressed against his was as rich as he remembered, or if time had painted everything with a glossy sheen. So what if just looking at her still sent shocks of amazement through him, and a longing so deep he felt it in his core?

So what, right? Because God knew, Noah was an expert at not getting what he wanted. He'd survived this long. He'd go on surviving.

He nodded again. "I'll expect you at ten o'clock on Monday."

"You're sure?"

"I'm sure. Welcome to the team."

She hesitated, then took his extended hand and shook it formally. And damned if that touch didn't send the entire rational and reasonable lecture he'd just given himself right into the goddamn shredder.

Fuck surviving, and fuck wondering. He wanted to know.

He wanted *her*.

Maybe he'd regret it. Maybe she'd slap his face. Hell, maybe she'd walk away from him and The Project and everything. But right then he knew in his gut that this was his best chance. Possibly his last chance. So when she started to pull her hand back, he tightened his grip and urged her closer.

"You said I shouldn't decide for you," he began. "I won't. I'm not."

Her brow furrowed. "What are you—"

"I'm leaving it to you. But I'm telling you flat out what I want. What I've fantasized about for years. I won't push. I won't demand. But just consider what I'm asking. Because I want this, and I think you want it, too."

She licked her lips, but she didn't pull her hand free. "You haven't asked me anything."

"No," he said, pulling her closer, desperate to claim her mouth with his own. "But I'm asking now."

CHAPTER 7

*O*H, *DEAR G*OD, *I'm melting.*

His mouth burns against mine as his hand cups my chin, holding me in place as he nips at my lower lip, taking exactly what he wants, and silently promising more. So much more.

And all I have to do is yield to him.

I can't. I shouldn't. I need to pull away.

Any other response and I'll regret this tomorrow. We both will.

Yes, maybe there is something between us— lingering attraction, intense lust, unfinished business, I don't know. But it doesn't matter, because we have to work together starting Monday, and this isn't good. It really, really isn't good.

Except it is.

It's so damn good.

He's like a drug, making my head spin. Stealing reason. Replacing responsibility with need and longing.

I slide my fingers up, then grasp his hair, and urge him even closer. If I'm in, I'm going to be all in, and I want no distance between us.

His teeth tug on my lower lip, and I moan, then part

my lips in response to his silent demand. He doesn't hesitate. His tongue sweeps into my mouth, claiming me, and I drink in the taste of him, all heat and male and decadent longing.

I don't know how long we're like that, glued together on the sidewalk in this shameless, passionate reunion, but it's long enough to provoke a smattering of applause and a few whistles. I pull back, feeling self-conscious and sheepish. But that emotion fades when I look at Noah's face. He's not embarrassed at all. On the contrary, he looks like he's just won the lottery, and it's more than a little humbling to realize that I'm the prize.

"Tell me that wasn't a tease," he says. "Because I'm not sure if I could stand it if you walked away right now."

I should—I know I should. But like before, any protest I might raise is beaten back by the ferocious intensity of my desire. I want him touching me again. I want to close my eyes and feel his hands on my body.

And I damn sure don't want to be on the street when he does that.

"My house is miles from here," I say. "Way South Austin. Where do you live?"

He turns and points at the steel and glass building that rises behind us.

I raise a brow. "You're kidding."

His smile is slow and very, very sexy. "Right about now, I'm thinking that condo was the best damn purchase I ever made."

"Right about now, I'm agreeing with you."

He takes my hand and leads me across the driveway

to the contemporary style entrance. Austin has a booming downtown area that's becoming known for its urban living. Most of my friends from the music scene can't afford a high-rise condo, but several of the clients and colleagues I've met through Crown Consulting live downtown, and I've seen the interior of a few of their luxury condos.

Noah's, however, is the first I've visited in this particular building. And his unit has, hands down, the best view of the river I've ever seen. "This is stunning," I say as I press my hands to the glass and look out at the sunset over the water. It's not quite six, but it's early November, and the world is illuminated in orange and purple as twilight engulfs the city.

I start to turn, but Noah rests his hands on my shoulders. "Wait. Just stay there."

There's heat in his voice, and my pulse kicks up in response. "Here?" I say, as his palms slide along my arms, so that his hands are over mine on the glass. He's moved closer, too, and now his body is flush against mine so that I can feel every inch of him. The brush of his hands. The hardness of his chest. The tease of his lips against my hair.

But it's the insistent pressure of his erection against my lower back that has me pushing against him, instinctively wanting to increase the contact between us as his hands begin a slow exploration while his mouth dips and his tongue teases the back of my ear.

"Noah." His name is a whisper. A moan. A plea.

"Did you think I wouldn't remember?" he murmurs. "Did you think I'd forgotten how this made you melt?

How I could take you right to the edge and then feel you tremble in my arms?"

I close my eyes, reveling in the sensation. In the heat that is spreading through me in response to his touch and his words.

With one hand, he tilts my head to the side, then kisses his way down my neck as his other hands slides under the white cotton tee I'd worn under my black blazer. I'd tossed the jacket over a chair as we'd come into the condo, and now I'm applauding my own forethought. I want nothing between us, and I'm relishing the sensation of his hand beneath the shirt and the electricity that shoots through me as he touches and explores.

He releases my head, then slides that hand down my body as well. Slowly, he peels up the shirt, then pulls it over my head and tosses it aside. I'm facing the window, and I can see our reflection. His mouth in my hair. His hands cupping my breasts through my lace bra.

"You're as beautiful as I remember," he says, tugging the cups down to expose my breasts. He takes one of my hands and lifts it, then positions my palm over my breast. "Touch yourself, baby," he demands, as he slides his hand down to the zipper on my slacks.

I close my eyes, rolling my own nipple between my thumb and forefingers. It's hard and sensitive, and I gasp as the need builds inside me. As his fingers dip lower and lower, first teasing me at the band of my panties, and then lower still until his fingertip strokes my clit, making me moan as I spread my legs, wanting more. Faster. Harder. Everything.

"Tell me you like that," he demands.

"I do."

"Open your eyes."

I obey, then hear my own shudder of excitement at the image reflected in the window. Me, with my legs spread and my pants still on, his fingers inside my fly as he teases me to the edge. My shirt, crumpled on the floor. My own hand, kneading and twisting my nipple, in a futile attempt to make the pressure grow, to make it bigger. Hotter. *More.*

My face, lost in need. Painted with desire.

And Noah, still fully dressed, holding me up, supporting me even as he is claiming me.

"I like that picture," he says, his fingertip still slowly circling my clit. "There's only one thing I'd like more."

I lick my lips, waiting. Trying to stand still. Trying not to shatter under the riot of sensations he's set loose in my body.

And trusting that whatever he wants of me next will take me that much further.

This is the Noah I remember. The man who held my pleasure in his hand. Who knew my body as well as I did.

A man who could set me on fire with nothing more than a glance. Whose fingers worked magic on me, and whose cock filled me. Whose words set my imagination soaring.

Slowly, he lowers his mouth to my ear again. And slower still, he whispers, "I want you naked."

A shiver cuts through me. I picture myself standing between him and the window. Seeing myself as he touches me. Feeling the brush of his clothes as he pulls me close. Vulnerable. *His.*

Boldly, I reach back and unfasten my bra, then let it drop to the floor. I'm wearing canvas flats, and I kick them off.

I hear him draw in a breath behind me. A simple thing, but the sound is just slightly uneven, and I know that he's as turned on as I am.

And that, frankly, makes it even hotter.

I keep my back to him, but my eyes are locked on his in the reflection. I lower my hands to my slacks. They're already unzipped, and now I slide my hand along the waistband, then shimmy out of them, finally kicking them aside.

For a moment, I stand defiantly in my underwear, as if to turn the tables and make him plead with me. But the truth is, I want this, too. I want to stand naked in front of him. I want to see the heat in his eyes as he looks at me.

That's the power I have, and I want to wield it. I want to bring him to his knees.

I want an explosion.

Because there's too much passion lingering between us. It's wild and it's dangerous and it's combustible. And until we burn through it, it's going to tie us together.

And as much as I wish we could get back to the past, I know it's not possible.

We have to get past this thing.

I know it; I'm certain of it.

But right now I'm so damn grateful that the only way clear is through the man himself.

Noah.

For right now at least, I'll take the moment. I'll take Noah.

And, I think as I peel off the panties and then stand naked in front of the mirror, I'll take as much of him as I can get.

"Kiki." His voice is low and reverent, and I draw a shuddering breath as I watch his face as his eyes trail down my reflection. My lips, slightly parted. My breasts, small but firm. And right now, with nipples as hard as pebbles.

He puts his hands on my waist and glides his palms over my silhouette. The curve of my hip, then the form of my thighs. And as he does, he lowers himself to his knees until I feel his mouth at the small of my back.

Gently, he turns me around, then pulls me close. I bite my lower lip in anticipation, then close my eyes as his thumbs trail slowly up my inner thighs, each pausing at the juncture, the pressure maddening, but in the best possible way.

I press my lips tight together, determined not to beg no matter how much I want to.

Then his mouth is there, his lips on my pubic bone, then lower over the smooth skin of my waxed mound. Now I'm biting my lower lip, and my legs are weak, and even without asking, I shift my stance, spreading my legs, inviting his touch.

His tongue flicks lightly over my clit, and I gasp, an electric-charged shudder running through me.

And that was just the beginning.

He repeats the motion, only this time he doesn't pull away. Instead, his mouth closes over my pussy, his tongue teasing and his mouth sucking. And there's no way that I'm going to win this battle. I have no choice but to find support in Noah, and so I bend forward, then clutch his head, both in order to keep myself steady, and to make sure that he doesn't stop. Not now. Not yet. Not until—

"Oh, God, Noah."

The cry is ripped out of me, my body breaking apart under the force of the explosion that came fast and hard. My hands are in his hair, twined with those fiery strands, and I force his head to stay in place, his tongue working its magic until the last gasps of the orgasm fade away, and I step back, breathing hard.

And, yes, wanting even more.

"You're still dressed," I say, an accusation in my voice.

He glances down at himself, then looks at me, his smile both playful and inviting. "So I am. What do you intend to do about that?"

I don't answer. At least not in words. Instead, I pull him to his feet, then step closer, so that I'm only inches away. Slowly, I unbutton his shirt, then push it off his shoulders before tugging down the sleeves and pulling it all the way off.

I let it fall to the floor, then press both of my palms against the hard planes of his chest. I slide my hands down, lower and lower until I reach his belt. I have it unfastened in no time, and I quickly unthread it.

I'm about to let it drop to the floor with the rest of our clothes when he shakes his head. "I don't think so," he says, and before I can protest, he's made the belt loop around itself, and tightened it around my wrists.

"What are you—"

"I think it's time we moved this party to the bed," he says, then gives the belt a little tug before he leads me that direction.

"On," he says, when we've crossed the studio, but I hesitate. The condo is a studio, so there are no interior full walls except around the bathroom. The bedroom area is in a corner, defined by the exterior walls of the studio, an interior halfwall, and a set of freestanding bookcases.

As we'd crossed the condo, I'd noticed a collection of framed photos on the far wall, and now I disobey Noah's order so that I can get a closer look.

Even across the room, they'd seemed familiar, and now I realize why. They're highly erotic images, but shot so beautifully there's no question but that they are art. In each photo, the model's face is hidden, but the pose and the posture are open and honest and full of blatant sexuality.

I've seen these images before, actually. They're prints from a traveling exhibit of work by a photographer named W. Royce, and I'd seen the show—*A Woman In Mind*—in Dallas, and thought it was brilliant.

"You have good taste," I say. "You picked some of his most exceptional prints."

Noah's eyes register surprise. "You're familiar with the show?"

"It's great."

"The photographer's a friend."

"Really? Well, tell him I'm impressed." I walk around

the bed so that I can get closer to one in particular. A woman with her hands bound to the bed, not with rope, but with a man's belt.

A warm flush spreads over my body, and my nipples tighten almost painfully.

I glance over my shoulder back at Noah. "Is that what you intend to do to me?"

He meets my eyes. "No." His fingers run over the leather of the belt. "That was just playing. Leading you to the bed."

"Oh. Why not?"

"You know why not."

He's right. I do, and I turn away, lost in a sudden memory. We'd played those kinds of games before. Nothing hard core, but lover's games. Handcuffs and ropes. Spanking. Once, even candle wax.

Games, yes, but the kind that require trust. Commitment.

And those are two things we've lost.

"Later," he says gently. But I know better. We'll never get to that point because this isn't a relationship. It's not going to grow.

On the contrary, tonight is a wall. A cure. A terminus.

The thought disturbs me more than it should, but I brush it off, then flash him a smile. "Good," I say. "Because right now, I need these hands."

Before he can ask what I mean, I give him a little shove onto the bed, then force him onto his back when I straddle him.

I make quick work of his slacks and shoes, and in no

time at all, he's naked beneath me. "There," I say. "That's better."

His eyes flash with green heat. "Much.'

He starts to say more, but I silence him with a kiss, then move my lips lower and lower, until my mouth is brushing over the smattering of hair on his chest, then down the straight line to his navel, and then down the final line of hair arrowing toward his very large, very ready cock.

I use my tongue only once, licking from his balls to the tip as I keep my eyes on his. "I want you inside me," I say, and am rewarded by his low, eager groan.

He edges sideways to get a condom out of the bedside table, then rolls it on. I approve, but at the same time it makes me sad. Because we used to be so far beyond that.

"Kiki?"

I realize I'm frowning, lost in the past, and I shift my expression, even as I shift my body to straddle him.

"Good girl," he says as I rub against him. I'm so wet already, my core clenching in anticipation. In want. In need.

"Touch me," I demand, and he strokes me, his fingers teasing my clit, then plunging deep inside me, making me wild. Desperate. Until I can't take it anymore and I lower myself hard and fast, taking him in, and then again and and again. Deeper and deeper until he's filled me, and I'm riding him, and I don't ever want to stop. Because this is Noah, and we fit.

We've always fit.

A momentary wave of melancholy crashes over me,

but then it disappears as rational thought is pushed out of my mind. Replaced by need and pleasure and vibrant passion.

Faster and faster I ride him, until finally he grabs my hips and slams me down hard.

I cry out, overwhelmed by the sensation of being filled so completely, coupled with the added friction against my clit.

A wild orgasm rips through me, turning me inside out, shaking me to my core as my body milks Noah and he explodes inside of me even as I tumble over the edge and burst into a million bright new stars.

I'M AS LIMP as a rag, utterly exhausted, completely drained—and I feel wonderful. We're spooned together, his arm draped over me, his chest against my back, and I'm breathing deep as I start to drift, anticipating reliving every delicious moment in my dreams since my body is too spent to survive another round in real life.

"This is what I wanted from the moment I saw you singing at The Fix," he murmurs, pressing a soft kiss to my shoulder. "But I never imagined we'd get here."

His words are innocent enough. And yet they rouse me back to consciousness, causing me to shiver as pinpricks of something akin to worry skitter over my skin.

"We can't," I begin, then let the words hang because I don't know where to go with them.

"I think we just did. And pretty well, too."

"No," I say, rolling over to face him. I draw a breath, gathering my courage. Because the truth is, I need all the strength I can muster to say what needs to be said. "No," I repeat. "This wasn't a beginning, Noah. It was an end."

He props himself up on his elbow, his brow furrowing as he studies my face. "What are you saying?"

I lick my lips. "That this isn't—this can't—go anywhere." He looks like he's about to speak, but I rush on. "You were right. There was a thing. Powerful, intense, and unresolved. That's what this was, Noah. What this had to be."

"What?"

"Closure."

His expression hardens. "And if I don't accept that?"

"Pretty sure this is the kind of thing we need to be in agreement on." I smile gently. Considering I'm still basking in the afterglow, I know that my words landed like a bomb in the middle of a garden party. "And besides, I start work for you on Monday, and I'm not fucking my boss."

He sits up, the sheet pooling around his hips. I look away. After what I've just said, I have no business ogling his abs or fantasizing about what's under the bed clothes.

"Technically, you're not an employee."

I cock a brow. "I have a reputation in this business, and I don't intend to tarnish it. But honestly, Noah, even if we were discreet, we both know that I'm right. Tonight wasn't a beginning, it was an end. Whatever we had before, it's long gone."

"Were you in the same bed I was? Because I don't believe that."

"I do." I blink, and tears spill from my eyes. "I'm sorry, but I do."

He reaches up, then gently brushes away my tears with the pad of his thumb. "Then we start over. We worked together once before. We got to know each other. We fell in love."

And then you broke my heart.

He's saying all the right words, but I can't erase the past any more than I can change it. It hangs over us like a flashing red warning sign telling me to beware. Reminding me that my heart isn't any stronger than it was all those years ago.

Warning me not to trust. Not to fall. Not to hope.

I did all those things before, and then he left, taking my heart with him.

He left, just like I'd known he would. Just like everyone does.

He left, and it destroyed me.

It's taken years to put the pieces of me back together, and now that I'm whole, I know better than to trust or to hope.

Noah Carter is a craving, nothing more.

And now that I've binged on him, it's time to push away from the plate, gather my self-control, and just say no.

"I'm sorry," I whisper, my voice thick with unshed tears. "I really am sorry, but it's time for me to go."

CHAPTER 8

NOAH COULDN'T SLEEP after she left, and the two fingers of the local Still Austin Bourbon Whiskey he'd downed weren't helping. He reached for the bottle, then stopped. Another drink wasn't going help any more than the first one had.

The problem was that she'd tied him up in knots, and it wasn't a familiar feeling. Women just didn't get under his skin. Not anymore. Not like that.

They hadn't for a long time. Years.

Not since Kiki, actually. And wasn't it ironic that here she was doing the same damn thing to him all over again?

From the first day that he'd met her, she'd filled his thoughts. The way she chewed on the end of her pen when she concentrated. The way she sweetened her iced tea with one splash of Diet Coke before offering him the rest of the can. The way she'd work late into the night rather than leave one tiny detail of a project hanging, but still managed to leave work far behind when it was time to play.

Even now, he could remember the look of surprise on her face when she'd finally stood up on his surfboard, then the way she'd sputtered with delight—not the least bit embarrassed—when she'd immediately fallen off again.

For months, it had been her smile that filled his mind whenever he closed his eyes. Her voice that urged him on, assuring him that all the time he was spending at the computer was going to pay off. That she believed in his talent, and that he was going to make a huge splash one day.

And he'd told her the same thing. He'd watch her pluck out a melody on her guitar, her voice adding words to the music that filled his apartment. He'd been amazed by the way she could sit and scribble out lyrics, profound and beautiful and sweetly sad, and then spend days and weeks massaging the words until what he'd foolishly believed was perfect grew into something transcendent.

He knew he had a gift for tech, but that was tangible, the numbers representing some physical property. The gift she had created emotions, and it both awed and fascinated him.

She'd filled him up back then. Her passion for her work underscoring his own. They'd worked hard and played hard. They'd fit together perfectly. And though he'd been so damn young back then, he'd believed that they would grow old together.

Then he'd gone and shot that fantasy all to hell, and suddenly Kiki wasn't in his life anymore. She was relegated to his memories, and he'd learned to live that way, like a man missing a limb.

But now she was back, filling his thoughts, and part of him wanted to run to her. To shake her. Kiss her. To make her understand that they'd had a second chance handed to them on a shiny silver platter. All they had to do was dig in.

But a bigger, saner part knew that she was right. They weren't the same people anymore. And while the attraction was there on both sides, the trust wasn't. She was skittish.

He got that.

He was the one who'd left, after all. He'd been an idiot, and he'd been paying the price for years.

Looked like he was going to keep on paying for a little bit longer.

Fuck.

It wasn't quite midnight, and since he couldn't sleep, he might as well work. By now, he should have received the latest reports on the prototype from the overseas production facility, and he could spend a few hours going through the evaluations and looking for functions that need to be tweaked before the final rollout.

That, at least, was a plan with two potential upsides. Either his concentration would be so laser-focused on the work that there was no room for Kiki in his brain, or else he'd fall asleep from the tedium.

Twenty minutes later, he was leaning toward the tedium side of the equation when his cell phone chirped, signaling a text message.

In Austin. My wife's abandoned me. You still up? More important, you up for drinks?

Noah grinned. Speak of the devil; he hadn't realized Wyatt was in town, and seeing the text now, when he could really use some company, was almost like a gift from the gods.

He tapped out a quick reply.

About time Kelsey realized she was too good for you. Come to my place. I've already downed two fingers for you. You're welcome.

Since he had no idea what part of the city Wyatt was coming from, Noah settled back at the desk, prepared to get in a bit more work done before his friend showed up. But his ass had barely hit the chair when he was startled by a loud rap on the door.

He pulled it open and found Wyatt standing right there. Which didn't say much for the building security, considering the elevators were operated by a six-digit password.

"What the hell? Were you waiting in the lobby?"

"Pretty much," Wyatt said, striding in. He was Noah's height, with golden brown hair and whiskey colored eyes that were crinkled with amusement.

"Where's Kelsey? Because if she's seriously left you, I should probably get word to her that I'm on the market."

"I'm meeting them at Griff's house later," Wyatt continued. "He's got a place in East Austin that he refurbished to turn a few of the rooms into a studio."

Now that Wyatt had mentioned it, Noah remembered hearing that Griffin was moving to Austin to work with a local production company that was producing his wildly popular podcast and adapting it to a web series.

"It's a pretty sweet set-up," Wyatt continued. "We drove his truck out from LA, along with the rest of his furniture."

"In other words, he owes you."

"Big time." Wyatt's smile reached his eyes. "I can trade on this for years."

"And if I hadn't been home?"

"That's the beauty of your new address. Such a convenient location. I would have just met up with them at whichever bar they landed at." He turned in a circle, taking in the open floor plan, the minimal furniture, and the collage of photographs on the back wall. "You've got good taste."

"Yeah, some asshole of a photographer twisted my arm until I bought some."

"The bastard."

Noah grinned. "How about that drink?"

Wyatt followed him to the kitchen, then parked himself on one of the stools tucked up under the breakfast bar.

On the way, Noah had grabbed his glass and the bottle. Now he pulled down a fresh glass for Wyatt and poured generously. "A local distillery," he said. "Welcome to Austin. And tell me how the hell you got to my door. Don't tell me the passcode lock is turned off on the elevators, because if it is, I'm having words with security."

"It's on."

"So, what? You opened the trap door and shimmied fifteen stories up the cable? Lyle's the action hero, not you. And even he needs a stunt man."

Wyatt spread his hands, looking smug. "I used your passcode."

"I never—"

"You didn't have to," Wyatt said, no longer with a teasing tone. "Anyone who knows you could make a solid guess."

Of course.

"Right," Noah said, his voice flat. "Pretty transparent." The code was the day, month, and year of his daughter's death.

"Oh, shit. Listen, Noah, I didn't mean to—"

"I'm fine. Really. So, you just came for Griff? Or do you have work lined up, too?" Even though Wyatt was kicking ass with his show, he still did some commercial work, and it wouldn't surprise Noah to learn that he'd come to Austin to take shots around the beautiful city.

It took Wyatt a moment to answer, and Noah was certain he was debating apologizing again for bringing up sad memories. Noah hoped he didn't.

Besides, he was the one who'd set that code, and he'd done it purposefully. Because he wanted that memory every time he rode the elevator.

He could live with the pain of losing Diana now. It had been torture at first, but the pain had dulled into a dark gray hole in his heart. What he couldn't live with—what he would never risk—was that a day would go by without at least one small memory of the little girl he'd loved so much. And so he had the code.

He kept his focus on Wyatt, who must have finally decided against apologizing, because he said, "No work for me, but on Monday, Kelsey's speaking to some local dancers about her experience in my show and filming *The Far Side of Jupiter*."

"That's wrapped, right?" Noah recalled that Kelsey's work on Wyatt's show had helped her land a role in a film adaptation of *Jupiter*, a Tony Award winning musical. "When's the release?"

"Not sure. Next year sometime. I guess I should probably know that." He frowned slightly, and Noah had to laugh. Not only did Wyatt's wife have a major role in the film, but Wyatt's own mother had worked on the screenplay and, Noah believed, acted as a producer. But despite Wyatt's deep Hollywood roots, he paid very little attention to the business. Hell, he'd gone so far as to change his name so that his status as Hollywood royalty wouldn't thwart his desire to make it on his own in his profession.

Wyatt sipped the bourbon, then slid off the stool. He crossed to the window and looked out over the now-dark river.

Noah took his own glass and settled into the big, ugly armchair. When he'd moved in, he hadn't had time to deal with furnishing the place, and so he'd let Carina hire someone for him, giving them free rein so long as they stuck to minimal, contemporary furniture.

But he'd insisted on keeping the chair. The ugly, battered, sore thumb of a chair.

He took a long swallow of his own drink and sighed with pleasure. For the first time since Kiki left, Noah finally felt relaxed.

Across the room, Wyatt turned away from the window, then leaned against one of the support beams while he looked back at Noah. "Okay, enough catching up. Pleasantries over, time to get real. You going to tell me what's up?"

So much for shifting gears. "What makes you think something's up?"

"Oh, let's think. You joked about being on the market—and yet you haven't been on the market since I met you. And you used Kelsey as part of the schtick, even though you had to know I'd either kick you in the balls or ask you what's wrong. So there you go," he added. "Now tell me what's up."

Noah hesitated. The truth was ... well, the truth was that he'd never told anyone the truth. Not even Kiki—not all of it. Maybe not even himself. Not fully, anyway.

But it was time. He needed to put it out there. Articulate his thoughts. Most of all, he needed someone to be his mirror. And if Wyatt dropping by tonight wasn't kismet, he didn't know what was.

"There was a woman," he began. "Before I married Darla, I mean." He drew in a breath. "She was ... hell, she was everything. It sounds lame, but—"

"It doesn't," Wyatt assured him, moving to sit on the couch opposite Noah. "Go on."

"I need to start from the beginning. I was twenty-four," he said. "I'd dropped out of college after my first year, because school was starting to interfere with my success. And by then I knew I'd made the right decision. I was mostly writing video games, but I was doing some innovative shit, and I'd gotten noticed. I was getting all sorts of offers to buy my little company."

"So you were going gangbusters," Wyatt said. "That I understand. Just stay away from the tech talk, and we'll be fine."

"I hired a lawyer and looked at the up and downside of selling—and ultimately decided to hold on to my little corner of commerce. I had the lawyers help me get some venture capital so I could expand into virtual reality and artificial intelligence, and that's when I met Darla. She was in college and working as a file clerk with my attorney's firm. We met, hit it off, started dating."

"Fell in love," Wyatt filled in.

"Honestly, no." Noah took another sip of his drink. Not so much because he wanted it, but because he needed the time. Had he ever admitted that out loud?

"No," he repeated. "We got along great. The sex was fine. We had a lot of the same interests, and we could go out to dinner and always find something to talk about. We started spending all our free time together. I don't know if she truly loved me, and to be honest, I never thought about it. Not really. One day she told me she loved me, and I said the words back. It felt like it was time." He looked at Wyatt. "Does that make sense?"

"Sure." He considered his answer. "I think so."

"Not your experience, though. Not with Kelsey."

Just the mention of her name made Wyatt's eyes brighten. His mouth curved up, and he said very simply, "No. Not with Kelsey. We were just kids, but she grabbed hold of my heart, and I damn well knew it." He met Noah's eyes. "I'm sorry you didn't experience that."

"I did. Just not with Darla."

Wyatt leaned back. "All right. Go on."

"Darla and I'd been dating about five months when I met Kiki. She's a musician, and she and some friends were starting a band. She'd blasted through UT in three years—she's originally from Texas—so she could race to LA to make it big, and she was doing some freelance scoring work at my company. She showed up at my desk, I took one look at her, and it felt like I was tumbling out into space."

From the look on Wyatt's face, Noah could tell that his friend understood the feeling.

"You got together."

"We did. We worked together for about a week, and we both fought the attraction every step of the way. Because otherwise it would be unprofessional, right? But then we gave in. One Friday we went out for Happy Hour, and midway through our second drink decided to officially call it a date. That date ended Monday morning when we both went back to work."

"And then you told Darla."

Noah nodded. "And then I told Darla." He drew in a breath. "She was hurt, but break-ups aren't supposed to be pretty and I was as gentle as I could be. The thing is, we probably would have gone merrily along if I hadn't met Kiki. I probably would have ended up proposing. We were comfortable, and—"

He shrugged. "Well, that was about it."

"A lot of people live their lives without a grand passion. Sometimes, maybe that's enough."

"Maybe. I don't know. I think it was enough for my mom."

"Your mom?"

Noah nodded. "My real father abandoned her when she got pregnant. Said he couldn't deal with being a dad and had no intention of getting married. She had me, struggled, and ended up marrying my stepdad when I was almost ten. He was a nice guy, and a great father, but they weren't a couple. They were two people who didn't want to be single. I wanted more. Hell, I wanted Kiki."

Wyatt went to the kitchen and returned with the bourbon, then poured them each another shot. "I already know how this story ends. You ended up with Darla. And the two of you had a baby. I'm guessing she told you she was pregnant."

"Yeah." Noah slammed back the entire drink. "*Fuck.* To this day, I don't know if I did the right thing or not. But I know it hurt like hell to do it. She told me the day after I proposed to Kiki. Can you believe it? We'd been apart for almost four months, and I was at the office, a little hung over because Kiki had said yes, and we'd done some serious celebrating."

He could still remember the way his head had pounded that day. He'd gone to the office even though it was Sunday to try to clean up some troublesome code, and Kiki was celebrating—and working—with her best friend, Celia. Their band, Pink Chameleon, had burst onto the scene after a single Kiki wrote blew the lid off both MySpace and YouTube.

That led to a manager and a record deal. They'd already been touring around the Southern California area, and they'd gained a pretty big following. But their new manager booked them for a national tour that was kicking off soon. The proposal had been in part because Noah wanted his ring on her finger before she hit the road with the band.

"So that Sunday, Darla came to my desk. She told me

she was almost five months pregnant. That she'd never been regular, and she didn't think anything of it until her clothes started fitting too tightly. She said she was scared. That she loved me. That she didn't make enough money to take care of a baby. She said she wanted her baby to have a father, and that she and I had been so good together.

"She said," he continued, his voice tight with emotion, "that she knew I was a better man than my father, who'd walked away from his responsibilities."

He lifted a shoulder, needing to get past this part of the story, because it hurt too damn much to think about it. "So I married Darla. I did the right thing." The word sounded like a curse.

"And that's the moment that my life went off the rails. That's the moment when I destroyed everything."

CHAPTER 9

NOAH FELT HIS body stiffen as the memory flooded back, heavy and gray and so full of guilt. The look in Kiki's eyes as he'd stumbled to get the words out. The raw, ripped feeling inside him because the last thing he'd wanted was to hurt her, and yet he couldn't stay. He couldn't walk away from Darla, from his child, and it was so damned unfair that she had to pay the price, too.

"I broke her heart—hell, I broke her spirit. She didn't even yell or cry. She just looked ... I don't know. Dead inside. Later, I saw an article that said she'd dropped out of the band after the first stop on their tour, and the words sliced right through me. I blamed myself, but I also knew I couldn't do anything—I couldn't even call her, because I was the last person she'd want to hear from."

He started to pace the room, needing to move, as if that way he could stay ahead of the memories. "After that, I couldn't bear to know what was happening in her life. I put up a wall. I shut out that part of my life. Because I knew I was doing the right thing."

"Your baby needed a father," Wyatt supplied.

"But it was more than that. I couldn't be what my

dad had been. I thought about being a weekend dad. Paying expenses. Bringing the child to my home with Kiki for weekends and holidays. But that wasn't fair to either the baby or Kiki."

"And you didn't think it would be enough, anyway," Wyatt said, with a perceptiveness that Noah appreciated. Guilt still clung to him, of course it did, but it was some small comfort to know that someone at least understood.

"It wouldn't have been. Not for me. I grew up hating my dad for walking away."

He forced himself to stop pacing and to meet Wyatt's eyes. To see the sympathy and the regret. "I just kept telling myself that I had to. That I couldn't be my father. That I had to take responsibility for the woman I'd gotten pregnant and the child I'd brought into this world. I hated myself for what I'd done. For what I was doing to Kiki. And all I had to hold onto was the belief that I was doing the right thing."

"Noah…" Wyatt's voice trailed off, as if he just couldn't find the words.

Noah stopped at the window, then looked out into the night. He'd destroyed so many lives by doing what he'd believed was the right thing. If he'd just stayed with the woman he wanted, Darla would be alive. Diana would be in school, growing up and breaking hearts. And Kiki would be his.

Stop it! The order was stern, and he pressed his forehead to the glass, willing himself to push down the guilt. But how could he, knowing what he'd destroyed?

He exhaled, his breath condensing on the glass. He watched it, focusing on the uneven edges as the condensate started to fade. "You would have thought the marriage would be awful, considering the circumstances. But it wasn't. I have to give Darla credit. And me, too. We worked hard. We really did. I didn't want to wear the ring only for show."

He moved away from the window and leaned against his desk, wanting the support that his work gave him. A tie to keep him from plummeting too far down into the past.

"And Diana," he continued, then fell silent as he gathered his words. Even now, his heart swelled when he thought of her. "She was the most beautiful baby in the world. I loved that kid like I never thought I could love anything or anyone. And smart. You could see it in her eyes. She saw everything, and I swear she understood most of it."

He closed his eyes, fighting back the swell of tears building in his chest, threatening to break out past the emotional dam he'd built so long ago. "She was almost one when the three of us went to Mexico City. I had a conference, and after that we were going to a beach resort."

"They were kidnapped," Wyatt said, and Noah nodded. Wyatt already knew that part of the story. He'd been there for Noah when, after seven long years, Darla had finally been pronounced dead.

"And now Kiki's back."

Noah dragged his fingers through his hair. "I'm that transparent?"

"I figured it was a good guess."

"I wasn't expecting to ever see her again," Noah admitted, "and then she's here."

"And there's still a connection?"

Without thinking, Noah's gaze shifted to the half-wall that separated the bedroom area of the studio from the rest of the space.

"I see."

"Then you have better vision than I do, because I've lost all perspective."

"What do you want?"

He lifted his hands and let them fall again, his whole body telegraphing frustration. "You and Kelsey—you were separated for about ten years, too, right?"

"Twelve," Wyatt said. "Twelve very long years, for which we are now very enthusiastically making up for lost time."

Noah laughed. He'd grown to love Austin, but God, he missed his friends. "How did you two bridge that time?"

"Are we your case study?"

"Pretty much," Noah admitted. "Consider yourselves my role models."

"In a word, trust." Wyatt shrugged. "We had to learn how to trust each other again."

Noah considered that. "When I first saw her here— in town, I mean—I almost let her go. Hell, I thought I *should* let her go. I was the one who fucked her over, right? No sense in bringing back painful memories. She deserved more, and I—well, I didn't deserve anything at all."

Wyatt looked purposefully toward the bed. "And yet…"

"And yet ... I couldn't make myself do it. I had to see her. Talk to her. I had to touch her, you know?"

"Oh, yeah."

"Even after all this time, I needed it. Wanted it." He shook his head, trying to order his scattered thoughts. "I still do."

"Does she?"

"She's wary. And we're working together now, which makes her even more leery. And she's very firmly put on the brakes."

Wyatt's brows rose. "You didn't mention the work part."

"Just one more complication in my screwed up life."

"What are you going to do?" Wyatt asked. A simple question, but it didn't have a simple answer.

"I don't know. She's right—we've changed. We're not the same people we were. And being together ... there's so much baggage. Guilt on my side, anger on hers. It's ... hell, it's just hard."

"And?"

Noah drew a deep breath. "You know what? Screw hard. I've gotten past hard more times than I can count. I want her. At the very least, I want the chance to see if we still fit. I want my shot."

"So take it."

"How?"

"I don't know," Wyatt admitted. "I guess you're going to have to get creative."

"FLOWERS," GRIFFIN SAID. "Inundate her with flowers."

Kelsey pushed a lock of brown hair off her face as she rolled her large, blue eyes. "That is *so* not creative. The man needs real help." She was sitting cross-legged on the flagstones in her brother's backyard. Griffin and Noah sat across from her in the Adirondack chairs, and Wyatt stood off to her right, leaning against a post.

Griffin shrugged as he turned to face Noah more directly, revealing the extensive scars that marred the right side of his face. The result of a horrific childhood injury.

"Flowers are awesome," Kelsey agreed. "But he needs to step it up. Oh! I know. *Edible* flowers." She looked at the three men and nodded, clearly proud of herself.

"What?" Wyatt asked. "Like the stuff chefs put in salads?"

"No, no. It's a thing now. Cookies that look like flowers planted in dirt that's really a brownie. God, I'm hungry. Griff, do you have any chips?"

He waved an arm. "Whatever's in the pantry, it's yours."

"I shouldn't eat this late," she said, rising. "But since we're brainstorming, we need sustenance."

Noah had to laugh. Here he was in his mid-thirties hanging out in the middle of the night in his friend's back yard to brainstorm creative ways to get a girl. Had anyone asked him yesterday if that was even a remote possibility, he would have told them he was too old for that shit.

But he couldn't deny that it was nice. Not only because he'd missed hanging out with his LA-based friends, but also because of the simple realization that they cared about him and Kiki. And, more, that they understood the guilt he felt—but were willing to tell him straight up to get over it.

Easier said than done, but he appreciated the thought.

After Noah had sliced open a vein and poured his heart out, Wyatt had decided they needed Kelsey and Griffin's input. Normally, Noah would have suggested they meet up the next day, but fueled by bourbon and friendship, he'd agreed to the late-night outing.

Also because of the bourbon, they'd called an Uber for the short drive into East Austin. Where—yet again fueled by alcohol—Noah had shared the story of his past with Kiki once more.

It was odd, actually. He'd held it so close to his chest for so long, as if there was no reason to take his past out and look at it. Now, though—with Kiki as his goal—it seemed natural, almost easy, to tell the story to his friends.

"Edible flowers aren't going to cut it," Wyatt said as Kelsey returned with a bag of Ruffles. "Not permanent enough. He needs something more tangible."

"Maybe," Kelsey said reluctantly. "But don't feel like you should avoid them as a gift—say, to your wife —just because she'll end up eating the evidence of your love."

Wyatt laughed. "Noted."

"You're such a freak," Griffin said, in response to which Kelsey wrinkled her nose at him. "And you're all missing the point," he added.

"Fine." Kelsey leaned against Wyatt, and he slid an arm around her waist. "Enlighten us, oh wise one."

Griffin turned to Noah. "You have to tell her a story. Nobody falls in love with a flower. They fall in love with your heart."

"You're the one who suggested a flower," Kelsey pointed out.

"And I was wrong," Griffin said. "Stop being so annoying."

"My irritating little brother has a point," she said, the laughter in her eyes making clear that, irritating or not, she adored Griff. "Not about me being annoying, but about the story. You need to catch her up on your life. You need to get to know each other again."

"We need to start over," Noah said.

Wyatt and Kelsey shared a glance. "Pretty much," Kelsey said. "But you get to start with a shared history." She bit her lower lip, then said gently, "Does she know what happened to Darla and Diana?"

He shook his head.

"I think you should tell her. Sooner rather than later. If you want to move forward, she deserves to know."

"Deserves?" he repeated. "She didn't deserve the hurt I caused by leaving. And now to pile this on? She must have hated Darla along with me. And now to learn that this happened?"

He dragged his fingers through his hair. "I wanted to keep the two paths of my life separate."

"You can't," Griffin said, flatly. "Because if you're going to let her see who you are now, you have to let her see what shaped you."

He knew that. He also knew that it was going to hurt. Him, and Kiki.

But maybe that was a good thing. He'd been numb so long, maybe he needed to hurt. Maybe that was just proof of life. And if he wanted Kiki in his life again, then by definition, he needed to start living again.

He stood up. "It's getting late, and my mind's going in circles. But I hear you."

Kelsey slipped away from Wyatt to give him a hug. "Good luck," she said. "We're here if you need us, even when we're in LA."

"Ditto," Griffin added. "And I'm almost always right here. The downside of working out of my house."

"And there's Sunday," Kelsey added, looking over her shoulder to Wyatt. "Right?"

"Absolutely."

"What's Sunday?" Noah asked.

"We're having a housewarming party here for Griff," Kelsey said. "Just a few friends. But you should come by. And," she added, with a sly smile, "you should bring a date. Or a work colleague if you need to spin it that way." She shrugged. "Basically, just do what you need to do."

What he needed to do.

He was still thinking about Kelsey's words as he rode in the back of the Uber. So far he didn't have a firm plan, but he intended to come up with one by tomorrow. The entire weekend was spread out in front of him, and he didn't intend to waste it.

He leaned his head back and closed his eyes, then realized that he hadn't checked his emails in hours. And while it was a long shot, she might have sent him a note.

Urged on by a tiny flicker of hope, he pulled out his phone and opened his mail app. Nothing from Kiki, but third in line beneath two bullshit ads, was a message from Damien.

Been talking with our potential competitors—they've experienced breaches from both inside and outside. Considering we're walking the same path, be sure to use precautions. We'll talk Monday. I'll have C put it on your calendar.

It was cryptic, but Noah could instantly see why. The Israeli company they were racing to the finish line was the victim of corporate espionage. And not only did they not think that Stark was behind it, but they feared that SATA might be vulnerable, too.

Noah wasn't too worried. He'd overseen the online security himself. As for the human element, that was trickier. But the office was still small, and he'd familiarized himself with most of the staff. It was possible that an outsider was getting in—someone from building security or the janitorial staff, maybe—but they'd still have to breach the system.

It was a puzzle, and not one he was going to solve in his current state of semi-inebriation. He'd grab some time this weekend to go to the office, though, so he'd be prepped for his call with Damien on Monday.

He was still thinking about the possibility of a leak when the car dropped him at home. Noah got out, then paused at the door of his building as he fumbled for his after-hours security card. As he did, he noticed a dark green pickup truck parked in one of the metered slots on the other side of the street, clearly illuminated by the line of street lamps.

Nothing unusual about that, except that there was someone sitting in the truck—a guy, or possibly a woman, in a baseball cap—and the someone turned quickly away when Noah looked that direction. And, Noah was certain, he'd seen a similar truck earlier in the day, when he'd held Kiki close and kissed her hard.

With a frown, he entered his building. He'd considered going over to the truck, but what would be the point? For all he knew, it was someone waiting to give a ride to a resident. Or a college student who'd been kicked out of his apartment, and was spending the weekend in his truck. There was no reason to think it had anything to do with Noah.

"Hey, Joe," he said, seeing the rail-thin man with salt-and-pepper hair reading the paper behind the security desk. The building didn't have full-time security, but Joe was a retired cop who did weekend rotations, doing walkthroughs and checking the security feeds.

"Mr. Carter, good to see you. I was just about to email you a report about the woman. Figured it was too late to buzz your unit."

Kiki?

"What woman?"

"Came in about twenty minutes ago looking for you. Pretty thing. Not that you could get the full picture with her hair all shoved up in a cap."

Frowning, Noah turned back to the entrance, but the truck had pulled away. "Did she say what she wanted?"

"Said she knew you, and that she wanted to know if this was your building. Said she wanted to see you again." His smile widened. "I told her that it's above my pay grade to give away any resident information, but that your name didn't ring a bell. I hope that was right. I know you like to be discrete."

In addition to working at the condo, Joe pulled a few shifts at various downtown hotels, and he'd seen Noah on more than one occasion with a woman. And never the same woman twice.

Noah frowned. He didn't know why one of his one-night stands would be hunting him down, but he was glad Joe had put the brakes on. He was never circumspect—he always gave a woman his card in case she needed to contact him. But that was an email address, not his home.

"You did the right thing," Noah assured Joe. The last thing he needed was a one-night stand deciding getting back together with him was her new pet project.

Especially since he already had a project of his own—Kiki.

CHAPTER 10

"**I** CAN'T BELIEVE you're not freaking out," Celia says, her voice surprisingly clear through the speaker on my mobile phone. "Matthew Holt has our track. Matthew. Fucking. Holt. Seriously, Kiki, how can you be blasé about that?"

"I'm not blasé," I assure her, catching Ares' eye. He and I are both sitting at my tiny breakfast table, and my phone rests near my picked over plate of chocolate chip pancakes. Celia—his cousin and my best friend—is about fifteen hundred miles away, having a not-so-quiet freak-out session in Culver city. "I just don't want to get my hopes up."

I can practically hear her rolling her eyes. "Dude, that's what hopes are for, you know? I mean, if Holt likes our track, who knows where it could lead? Actually, fuck that. It could lead to a Grammy. Worldwide tours. Licensed Pink Chameleon merchandise available in a department store near you."

"She's right," Ares says. "Soon, you too might be an action figure."

"You're such an ass," Celia tells him, and I start laughing.

"All right," I say. "You win. I'm super-duper excited about the fact that you had a friend of a friend slip Holt a CD that is even now probably sitting in a cardboard box filled with similar CDs that will very soon be transferred to his secure vault. Otherwise known as his trashcan."

"You, my friend, are a downer. And we didn't send a CD. We sent a digital file. To his *personal* email address. Come *on*, Kiki. This is awesome, and you know it."

She has a point. Holt has serious clout in the industry. He's a triple threat, and his company—Hardline Entertainment—has fingers in the music, film, and television industries. He has a reputation for being reclusive, dangerous, and brilliant. Some of the wilder rumors even say that he killed a man, but I think that's PR-driven hype. He doesn't sign many bands, but the ones he anoints inevitably climb the charts fast. And if Celia really has managed to get our music in front of him, that's one hell of an amazing feat.

I give in with a laugh. "Fine, fine! It's cool. And my fingers are totally crossed." I draw a breath. "I'm sorry for yanking your chain. I'm just—"

"Afraid someone's going to pull the rug out from under us?" she supplies. "Certain that the universe has it in for you? Convinced that every time your fingers touch something you want, it'll be ripped away from you?"

I swallow. She's hit a little too close to the mark.

Apparently, she realizes it, because the next thing I hear is her soft curse, followed by, "Oh, hell, Keeks. I'm sorry. Forgive me?"

I picture her biting her lower lip, her model-pert

nose scrunched up as she waits for my answer.

"Fine." I say. "You're forgiven. So long as you stop calling me that."

"Phhhbt. It's cute. It suits you."

I glance at Ares, who looks toward the ceiling and shakes his head in exasperation. "The woman runs her own high powered marketing company," he says. "You're really going to saddle her with *Keeks*?"

"Hey, I think it's great that your consulting gig is doing so well, but right now we should be focused on the band. Seriously, you ought to move out here. It'll be easier to record more tracks."

"What track did you send Holt?" I ask, intentionally changing the subject.

"*Back to You*," she says, referencing the song I sang Wednesday night at The Fix. It was the first song I'd performed on stage in years, but not the first I've written. It took me years, but once I picked up my pen again, I realized how cathartic it was.

Now, I have quite a collection, and we've been culling through them, picking the best to score together. Kristi and Eden—the other two members of the band and my second best friends next to Ares and Celia —are both doing studio work in Nashville through the end of the year. But they come to LA at least once a month, and when they do, the three of them record the music and their vocal parts in LA. I record my vocals here at the studio Ares uses. And then Celia edits it all together. She's not a sound engineer, but she's done a damn fine job on the three demo tracks we've pulled together so far.

"I'm serious," she says, ignoring my change of subject. "You should move back here. We could re-launch Pink Chameleon so much faster if you were closer. You wouldn't even have to stop consulting. There are plenty of places out in LA that need a kick-ass marketing consultant."

I meet Ares eyes, looking for support, but he just shrugs. "Don't look at me. But if you are going to quit, then I think you should tour with Seven Percent. It's only a few months, and it would get you back in a performance rhythm."

"You're just frustrated because some of your new material really needs a female lead singer," I say.

"I admit it openly," he says. "Just tour with us for a month—even a few weeks. We can audition replacement girls on the road."

I let out a frustrated groan. "You guys, come on. I like my job, and I like Austin. Besides, LA is freaking expensive, and I'm living mortgage-free here." Cam and I had inherited Gram's house, where I now live alone, since Cam rented a place closer to campus. "And, the whole point of working and living on the cheap is so that I can stockpile money to live on so that I can focus only on the band when I *do* move out there." The *when* being once Kristi and Eden are back, and once we've got enough songs ready to go that it makes sense to book some studio time to record the tracks, start releasing them, and get serious about finding a tour manager.

"Plus," I continue, because now I'm on a roll, "I need Maia to be up to speed on Crown Consulting. She's got great ideas and works well with clients, so she could hold the business together for a few months. But she's still green, and I want her on this current Stark job with me. Because then—*when, not if*—Pink Chameleon goes on tour, she can babysit Crown Consulting and I don't have to worry that the business I built is going to crash and burn just because we're getting the band back together."

"Oh, please. Your business is going to be bigger than ever. Because you'll be the one promoting the shit out of Pink Chameleon."

"True," I say. "But why is it always on me to go to you? Why don't you come here? Austin. Music. They kind of go together, remember? We can work on band stuff while I finish this job. It's got a tighter time frame than I thought, so I should be clear by early next year."

I don't mention that I'll have little to no free time. I know Celia well enough to know she's not going to jump on that offer.

"You want me to give up the beach for Texas? Yeah, no. We'll stick with the plan. It's just that I'm really not a patient person."

That's such an understatement, I burst out laughing. "Believe me, I'm well aware. And I'm excited about getting Pink Chameleon back together, too," I assure her. "But I have to do this right. I screwed up my music career once before. I don't think I'll get a third bite at the apple if I screw up this chance, too."

"*You* didn't screw up," she says loyally. "The rat bas-tard screwed you up. Huge difference." The rat bastard, of course, is Noah. And starting Monday, I'm going to be working side-by-side with him.

"What?" Ares is peering at me, his brow furrowed in question.

I shake it off. "Nothing," I lie. But the truth is that the enormity of that fact just hit me. *Side by side with Noah.*

My insides do a tumble, and I swallow back a nervous laugh. Maybe Celia is right. Maybe I need to turn down the job and get my ass to LA.

Except I can't. I really do need the money. And I really don't want to leave Maia in charge until I'm sure she can handle it.

And, if I'm being really and truly honest, I don't want to leave Austin—or Stark Applied Technology. Not now.

Because maybe I secretly kinda, sorta want to be around him.

And that's true even if leaving would be better for my heart.

In California, Celia releases a long, loud sigh of resignation. "Okay, fine. But when Holt goes gaga over our stuff and wants to meet us in person, you're flying your ass out here."

"Damn right, I am."

"Okay, then. I'm going to go get some breakfast. Have a good weekend," she adds. "But not too good. You owe me new lyrics. We had a pact."

"I know, I know. Go. Let me work."

We'd agreed to get one new song ready every two months. Faster if we could. And I haven't sent her fresh lyrics in over three weeks. What can I say? Prepping for the Stark proposal ate up almost all of my spare time. And now that I have the job, the work is going to devour the rest of it.

I push back from the table. "She's right. I need to park myself in my room and finish up *Starfall*. What are you up to today?"

"Me and the guys are doing a whole slew of videos that Tanya can post during the tour." Tanya is the drummer's wife, and Seven Percent's social media manager.

Ares stands and starts to clear the table. "Before you disappear into your cave, tell me what's up."

"Up?"

"When Celia mentioned the rat bastard—you flinched."

"I did not." *Shit*. I probably did. "You're imaging things."

"I don't think so." He scrapes the pancakes into the trash, then drops the dishes into the sink with a clatter.

"It's just that we're going to be working together." That's true, of course, but it's not the whole truth. And I'm not ready to share how much Noah is messing with my head and my heart.

He studies me for a moment, and it's clear he doesn't believe me. But he holds up his hands in surrender. "Fine. You don't want to tell me, I'm not going to pry."

"There's nothing to tell," I say, as the doorbell rings. "Oh, hell. That's probably Mr. Fowler."

My neighbor is the epitome of a crotchety old man, and his biggest pleasure in life is calling me out when I forget to roll my trashcan to the backyard after trash day. Apparently, my oversight not only destroys the beauty and serenity of the neighborhood, but sucks the pleasure from life itself.

"Then he's more off his rocker than usual," Ares says. "I pulled it back on my way in last night."

"You did?" I pause at the door and turn back to him with a smile. "Thanks."

I'm already tugging the door open when I turn back, only to find Noah Carter standing once more on my doorstep.

"Noah!" His name slips from my lips, and I stand frozen like an idiot, my hand still on the knob.

He's dressed casually. Jeans with canvas loafers, paired with an open gray button down over a pale blue T-shirt. He's clean-shaven, and though I imagine he started the day with his hair combed, now it's ruffled. From his fingers, I'm sure, but it suggests a day at sea. And, frankly, it's undeniably sexy.

I give myself a quick mental kick in the ass, because that is not the direction my thoughts need to be going.

He's wearing aviator style glasses, which means I can't see his eyes. He's probably looking me over, and right then I wish I was wearing anything other Disney PJs under a fluffy robe covered with embroidered pink ducks.

I frown up at him, hoping my stern glare makes up for my ridiculous outfit.

Probably not my smartest move, though, because the moment he tugs the sunglasses off, I melt a little, caught up in the green fire of his gaze. My heart skips a beat, and the corner of his mouth curves up, as if he knows exactly what I'm thinking.

I take a step back and force myself to rally. "I didn't think I'd see you until Monday." I make the words harsh. Accusatory.

As they should be. After all, I thought I'd made it clear that ours would be a business only relationship.

"I need your thoughts about something," he says. "It can't wait."

"Oh." I lick my lips. I'm a professional, so I'm hardly going to send him scurrying just because I'm not official- ly on the clock. Of course, I would have preferred an email. My porch is no place to debate communication methods.

"Go on," I say without moving. I've decided not to invite him in. Not unless the question requires discus- sion. "What is it?"

He peers at me, his serious expression softened only by the hint of a smile at the corner of his eyes. "When was the last time you played miniature golf?"

CHAPTER 11

"MINIATURE GOLF?" I repeat, trying to make those words fit into some sort of context. It's no use. I've got nothing.

"When was the last time you played?" he presses. "A year? Two? Do you go every Saturday?"

"Um, college, probably." I push the door open all the way so that I can lean on it as I watch him. He's still on my porch, which doesn't seem to faze him at all. At the same time, Ares passes into view, moving from the breakfast nook toward the bedrooms.

He pauses in front of the door, his dark eyes like question marks. "Everything okay, there?"

"Fine," I say, glancing at Noah, who's looking at Ares, his eyes narrowed in a scowl.

I shift my attention back to Ares. He's wearing boxer shorts and a Keep Austin Weird T-shirt. He's ridiculously good-looking, with his midnight black hair and gray eyes.

I press my lips together, relishing the moment. Because unless I'm way off base, that's jealousy I see in Noah's eyes.

Not that I'm contemplating anything but work between Noah and me, but a girl's got her pride. And, after all, there was last night … even if I did walk quickly and firmly away.

Ares realizes it too, and he shifts his gaze from Noah's face to me, his brows rising in amusement. *Go,* I mouth, and he takes one final look at Noah, then complies with my silent demand.

Noah watches him go, then turns his attention back to me. "So, are you and he—"

I narrow my eyes as I gesture him inside. "*Now* you ask if I'm involved with someone?" I say as I close the door. "I showed up at your office with a different last name, and yet I don't recall any conversation about a significant other before…"

I trail off, because I can feel my cheeks heating, and I don't want him to notice. Instead, I turn my back to him and lead him toward the kitchen. "Coffee?" I ask.

"Before coffee?" he repeats, and I know he's teasing. "You're right. There was no discussion about significant others before coffee," he agrees. "Or before sex, for that matter."

"Sit," I say, pointing at the table, which Ares has wiped down. As houseguests go, I have to give my temporary roomie his props.

"You want honesty?" he asks.

"Always."

"I knew you were divorced. After your interview," he explains. "I looked you up."

"Oh." I think about that, trying to decide if it's creepy or flattering.

I go with the latter, but only because it was Noah

doing the looking.

"You still haven't answered the question," he says.

"Yes, I did. College. I haven't played miniature golf since then."

"About him," Noah clarifies, pointing vaguely in the direction of the bedrooms. "The guy with the band."

"Ares," I say. "His name is Ares Sanchez."

"Tyree called you his girlfriend."

"He did?"

"Is he?"

"That's not really your business," I say.

"Is he?" Noah repeats, his voice tight, almost as if the answer could hurt him.

For a moment I consider telling Noah that we're involved. It would be a lie, but it would make everything so much easier. I could say we'd had a fight and I was vulnerable, and that's why I slept with Noah. But that everything is back to normal now, and Ares is my guy and Noah is my boss.

It's a solid plan. It would put up a nice clean barrier between us, one that would erase any *what ifs,* and make it so much easier to focus on work. To sweep the past away so that we didn't have to deal with any lingering emotions at all. Because why bother settling old hurts or rekindling buried desire if there's no end game?

Yet I can't make myself say the words. I want easy— I do. God knows my past with Noah was hard enough to last a lifetime. I should be jumping all over the chance to shut this down—whatever *this* is.

But I don't. I can't.

And I'm not sure if it's because I can't bring myself

to drag Ares into a lie—or because I don't want to put up those barriers.

"We're not dating," I say, then turn away from him as I pour myself a cup of coffee. "You never answered my question either. Do you want coffee?"

"No thanks. I had some at home. I'm cutting down."

I face him, cradling my cup instead of holding it by the handle. It's hot on my palms, and it gives me something to focus on other than how he looks so at home sitting at my table. Like we do this all the time, just spend a weekend morning in the kitchen talking. "Orange juice?" I offer.

He shakes his head but says nothing.

"We're not even roommates," I add, though why I need to clarify that, I have no idea. I'm probably just rambling to fill time. "He's just staying here because Seven Percent doesn't leave until Monday, and he's already leased out his place for the length of the tour."

"Oh." I see the tiniest hint of a smile touch his lips, as if he's fighting hard not to grin. "Well, I hope the tour goes well."

"It will. Their band is rock solid," I add, then bite back a little chuckle.

"What?"

I shake my head. "Nothing. If Ares were in the room, I'd be teasing him about how they need a female lead singer."

"And that's funny because…"

"He's asked me to tour with them. It would just be my way of giving him shit." I meet Noah's eyes, then quickly look away. I'd forgotten how easy it is to just talk to him, and I'm not entirely sure why the feeling that we're sliding back into a rhythm makes me nervous.

I point to the Keurig coffee maker behind me, deliberately shifting gears. "You sure you don't want some? I have decaf."

"Yeah, okay. Why not? So why aren't you?" he asks as I start a cup for him.

It takes me a second to realize he means the tour and not the coffee. "Well, for one thing, it would be hard to work for you if I was on a stage in Deep Ellum," I say, referencing a club-filled area in Dallas where I know Seven Percent is playing first.

"I'm not saying you should go—trust me, after interviewing everyone else, I'd be doubly sad if you decided to skip out."

"Doubly?" I ask, putting his coffee on the table and taking the seat across from him.

"I want you here," he says plainly. "And not just because of work."

"Oh." I take a sip of coffee. He's spoken pretty damn clearly, but I'm still not sure how to interpret that. But I'm also not going to ask.

"What I meant was that I'm surprised your business is marketing now. That's all. When we—I just mean that you were always focused on the music."

"Right." His words hurt more than they should, but they've brought back a flood of memories. Because Noah had always been my biggest champion, encouraging me and Celia to take Pink Chameleon as far as it could go.

And then he left, and I crumbled, taking the band

with me.

"Kiki?"

I exhale through pursed lips, as if I'm doing some sort of meditative breathing exercises. "You don't know?" Then I shake my head. "No, why would you? I didn't try to follow your life either, after—*shit*." I push back from the table and stand, furiously blinking away the tears that now sting my eyes.

He's on his feet immediately, then at my side before I can fully prepare myself. "Kiki," he says, then presses his hand tentatively on my shoulder. Even that light a touch is too much for me, though, and I shrug it off. I step away, needing to keep my back to him as I gather myself.

"Do you want me to go?"

I suck in a lungful of air, then another. Finally, I turn around to face him, my wits restored. "No. I'm fine. It just hit me all wrong."

"I didn't mean—"

"I know you didn't."

Slowly, gently, he reaches out and touches my hair, and it's all I can do not to move closer. To let him pull me into his arms and hold me. I want that—but at the same time, I don't. I really don't.

"Please," I whisper. "No."

"I never stopped loving you," he says. "I know I hurt you—and, God, I wish I could take it back—but I never stopped loving you."

"Don't." I look at him through eyes damp with tears. "I don't want to relive the past. I survived it. I got through it. But I sure as hell don't want to go back to it."

I lick my lips and lift my chin so that I can see his eyes. "And even if what you say is true, the girl you never stopped loving isn't me. Just like the guy I once loved isn't you."

I see him flinch, but I don't slow down. "It's been years, Noah. A lot of years. Things change. People change. *We've* changed. Last night, we had our moment of closure—"

"Moment?" he says, and despite myself, I laugh. He could always do that—lighten a heavy moment so that it was that much easier to bear.

"Fine," I correct. "We had a few amazingly blissful hours of closure, but that's all it was. Shutting the door on the past. Because the truth is, we don't really know each other anymore."

"Do you think I don't realize that? I don't want to go back, Kiki. These last years have included some of the worst moments of my life. I have no interest in reliving any of that. What I want is to go forward. What I want is a second chance."

"I already told you I'm not sleeping with my boss." I say the words more firmly than I need to, as much a reminder to myself as to him.

"Then I guess it's a good thing that I'm suggesting we start fresh as friends." He flashes a quick, mischievous grin. "And I'm not even suggesting friends with benefits. Unless, of course, that appeals to you."

I try to scowl, but I can't help laughing. "Friends?"

He spreads his hands and grins. "I came here with nothing on my mind but miniature golf. Come on," he says. "Let's go. Or we could sit here and poke over our past in minute detail. Personally, if we're going to catch up, I'd rather do it while trying to knock a small ball into a tiny cup."

I press my fingers to my lips to hold back a snort of laughter. "Couldn't have said it better myself," I manage. I glance down at my less than attractive pajamas, and for the first time, I wonder about the state of my hair. And my face, for that matter. I fell asleep in my makeup last night, so I probably look like a raccoon after a bar fight.

Then again, I guess that says something for Noah. After all, he didn't back off in shock when I first opened the door.

"I'm going to go change," I say. "Help yourself to another coffee."

I head back to my bedroom, pausing to tap on Ares' door, then poke my head in when he grunts permission. "Hey, I'm going to go out with Noah."

"Are you?" His brows rise with interest. And, I think, amusement.

"It's not like that. We're going to be working together. It's smart. Get past any lingering awkwardness before we're stuck in close quarters working through marketing plans."

"Mmm-hmm."

I roll my eyes. "Just relaying the info in case you're looking for me later."

"Have fun," he says, with such a tease in his voice that I can't resist lifting my middle finger in response.

He laughs. "I think you're aiming that suggestion at the wrong man."

Since I clearly can't win, I just shut the door and

head to my room to change. But I'm smiling, and I know it's because of Noah and the day that's spread out in front of us.

I also know I have to be careful; this man has the power to hurt my heart. I know that. But knowledge doesn't control feelings, and even though part of me wishes I could deny it, the truth is that being around him makes me feel happy.

And all I can do is hope to hell that he doesn't hurt me again.

CHAPTER 12

"I'M THREE UNDER par," I say as I gently tap my ball with a putter and try to send it straight between the legs of a giant Tyrannosaurus Rex. "You were right. I'm seriously kicking your ass."

I smile sweetly at Noah, who hasn't managed to sink any ball within the prescribed number of strokes.

He leans on the end of his putter. "Hey, no ego here." He meets my eyes. "My talents lie in different areas."

Heat floods my cheeks, and I look away, ostensibly following the direction of my ball. "That's good," I say, lightly. "Because you won't be making a career of miniature golf."

Not that Austin's iconic Peter Pan Mini Golf center is typical miniature golf. With the statues of Peter himself, Tinkerbell, giant whales, and whatnot, its focus is more on whimsy than skill.

When Noah had first pulled into the parking lot on Barton Springs Road, he'd smiled proudly at me. "Every article I've read since I moved to Austin says this is a can't-miss place. Have you been?"

He'd so obviously done his homework that I hated

to burst his bubble, but every Austinite knows about this place. And even though I was already twelve when our mother left Cam and me with Grams and hit the road, I still consider myself an Austinite. Mostly because I have no interest in remembering those early years in Waco at all.

"I had my thirteenth birthday party here," I'd told him. "And my friends and I came at least once a month in college."

"Damn," he says. "And I wanted to be different."

Now, as we're well into the course, I grin at him with genuine pleasure. "This was a really great idea," I say. "I've been spending so much time inside, I'd forgotten how nice a day out in the world can be."

"What's kept you trapped?" he asks as I retrieve my ball, and we move on to the next hole.

"Planning for your consult, for one. But mostly writing music. The girls and I are breathing life back into Pink Chameleon."

"Yeah? That's great." He lines up his ball and shoots.

Across the way, some kids at a birthday party squeal when someone gets a hole-in-one by a giant bunny.

"And that reminds me," he says, after he's finally sunk his ball seven strokes later. "You never answered my question. Why marketing? And what happened to Pink Chameleon that you have to get it back together?"

"You really didn't pay attention." I look up from where I'm about to hit the ball, and see that he's looking hard at me.

"Attention?"

"To me," I clarify. "All these years between us, and

you never tried to find out what I was up to?"

His expression takes on a hard edge. "I wanted to," he admits. "Pretty much every damn day."

"Why didn't you?"

He leans on the end of his putter. The intensity has faded from his face, and when he meets my eyes, I'm struck by a sadness so palpable it's all I can do not to walk to him and take him in my arms.

"Do you have any idea how hard it was walking away from you?" he asks. "Do you think I don't know how much it hurt you?"

"Did you?" I hate how needy I sound, but I am. Hearing this is like a balm for my soul, healing the wounds I'd inflicted on myself, believing that the connection between us had been an easy one for him to break, and that he hadn't suffered the way I had.

"Oh, God, Kiki, I hate that you can even ask that. It was fucking torture. But I had to do it. I couldn't walk away from my child. You know that. You know why I left."

I press my lips together, willing myself not to cry out to him. To tell him that maybe he could have. Not abandon the child, but provide for it. Monetarily and emotionally. To scream that we should have talked about it—really talked about it. That we'd been a couple, and I'd deserved to be part of his decision, not the unhappy recipient of a horrible pronouncement.

"I don't know," I admit. "I guess it seemed so easy for you. The way you came to me once she told you about the baby. You already had a plan. It was all mapped out like a goddamn math equation."

He winces, but doesn't argue. All he says is, "It was hard. Walking away from you was the hardest thing I've ever done. And even though there were times when I craved just a hint of you—just the tiniest glimpse of your life—I never looked. I thought it would hurt too much.

"So there you go," he says. "That's why I didn't poke into your life until yesterday, when I looked you up to find out about your marriage. And I'm guessing that you didn't try to find out what I was up to for similar reasons."

I swallow—he's so very right—then hit the ball. I miss the cup by a mile.

"What's the story?" he presses, as I line up my putt again.

I want to tell him it's none of his business. I don't want to admit the truth to him. The truth would be a confession of weakness. More than that, I'd have to reveal just how much power he had over me back then.

"I'm sorry," he says, obviously understanding my hesitation. "You don't have to tell me anything."

Part of me wants to stay quiet, but a bigger part wants to clear the air. And without conscious decision, I start talking again. "After you left, I couldn't write. I couldn't sing. I was numb. Everything creative in me died."

I hit the ball, and it goes straight into the cup. I barely notice. "I dropped out of the band," I tell him. "And after a while the girls went their own ways, too."

"Celia?"

It touches my heart that he still remembers my best friend's name. "She understood. It sucked, but all the girls got it. It wasn't fair, and I told them to bring in someone else, but…" I trail off, then lift a shoulder. "They didn't, and it fell apart, and I've always hated that I didn't have the strength to work through it for them. For the band."

"Hated me, you mean." There's no accusation in his voice. Just guilt.

I shake my head. "No. Really, *no*. I understand why you left. She was pregnant, and you couldn't stand the thought of being an asshole like your dad. I hated you at the time, yeah. But I understood. I thought you were wrong, and I was pissed as hell. But I understood."

I pull my ball out of the cup. "And I should probably say that now that you're divorced, I also feel weirdly vindicated. I knew you shouldn't have married her, and I was right. But like we already said, that was a long time ago."

I lift my shoulders in a combination of apology and *what can you do,* and am struck by the odd, unreadable expression on his face. "Noah?"

He shakes his head. "Just thinking." His voice sounds unusually hoarse. "I'm glad to know you didn't hate me," he adds, and I decide that his odd tone is a reflection of deep emotion. "Go on. You were telling me about the music."

"Right. Well, it took me a long time to get over that. Honestly, I've only been writing again for about a year. After you went to Darla, I moved home and got my MBA in marketing. I love it. I really do. But I love music more."

"Which doesn't explain why you're not touring with

Ares, now that you're not blocked anymore."

This time, he sinks the ball in two shots, and as he comes closer to retrieve the ball, I reach up and he high-fives me. Except he doesn't really, because when his hand hits mine, he doesn't then pull it back. Instead, he holds on, squeezing my hand for just a moment, before releasing me.

I frown, not sure what that was for, but knowing that I liked the sensation of my skin against his.

"Kiki?" he asks, as if he has no clue that his touch has scattered my thoughts.

"Oh, right. That's because of Pink Chameleon." I explain how the girls and I have been working on our songs, and how I plan to use the money from the Stark gig to live on while we give the PC reboot a go. "Do you think that's foolish?"

"Hardly, I think it's great. Watching you on stage the other night—it's your element." His mouth quirks into a grin. "Not that I want you to back out on the Stark contract. We need you. On the whole, I guess you're just too damn talented."

I laugh, enjoying his teasing more than I should. And, more than that, I'm relieved and flattered by the fact that he seems to genuinely mean what he says. And that he doesn't think that following this dream so late in the game is foolish.

There's a bench nearby, and he goes and sits down as a couple with three little kids start to play through. "Listen," he says. "You mentioned me being divorced…"

My gut twists as I nod. Surely they're not still married? I'm certain he said he wasn't with her.

"You should know we never got divorced. I'm widowed."

"Oh." The news is like ice water. I'd thought he left her. I'd thought that he realized it was a mistake to be with her. "I see."

I suck in air, trying to rearrange my thinking. Honestly, what difference does it make? She's out of his life. And I'm not in it, either. Not like that, anyway.

"Do you have custody of the child?" I realize I have no I idea if he'd had a boy or a girl.

"Diana." He swallows, and an expression that looks like pain cuts across his face. "She's dead, too."

"Noah…" I take his hand and hold it tight. "I'm so sorry. Was it an accident?"

"She was murdered. They both were."
A cold feeling washes over me, so intense that for a moment I actually think that a November cold front has blown in. "That's horrible." The word is completely inadequate. "I—I don't know what to say," I admit.

"I almost didn't tell you. It shouldn't be your burden. But…"

"Yes?"

"I meant what I said. I want us to start over. That's in my past. That's a huge part of my past. And like it or not, it's tied to you, too. So you needed to know."

"I'm glad you told me. Do you want to tell me what happened?" I'm not sure I want to know, but I'm glad I asked, because he tells me the story, and I think it's cathartic. For both of us.

He lays out the whole thing, his voice monotone,

and I tremble as the story turns worse and worse. The trip to Mexico. The afternoon that Darla and Diana didn't come back to the hotel. His fear. The news that Diana had been found.

"I shut down, that day," he says. "For a long time, I was sure I'd never heal. Honestly, I'm not sure I ever did."

I don't know what to say, so once again, I just hold his hand as he continues talking about the investigation and how helpless he felt. About the search for Darla. And how, much later, he got involved with a covert vigilante-style organization called Deliverance that helped locate and rescue kidnap victims. Not because he thought he would find Darla—he looked, yes, but by then, he was almost certain she was dead—but because he wanted to help other families. Other victims.

And, ultimately, about how he had to quit Deliverance. Because even though he knew he was helping others like himself, the constant memory was making him feel dead inside.

"I never had a chance to let the wounds heal," he told me, and I tried to imagine what it would be like to constantly relive your pain.

"And they never found Darla's body? That must make it so much worse."

He nods. "She's been pronounced legally dead, so that's some closure. But it's hard." His eyes meet mine, then cut away quickly. "It wasn't a great marriage." His voice is low, like he's sharing a secret. "But we were both trying. And it was getting better. Diana was like a talisman that made us closer. We'd gone to Mexico so I could go to a conference, but they came with me because we'd been doing so much better, and we wanted to be a family."

He looks back at me, and I see the apology in his eyes, as if that confession hurts me.

"Don't." I clutch his hand tighter. "Do you think I wished a horrible marriage on you? I didn't, I swear. I told you I understood, and I meant it. I felt sorry for myself, and I was angry, but I never wished that you were stuck in a bad marriage. And I sure as hell would never wish something like this on you. On anyone."

"I know," he says, then reaches out and brushes my cheek, wiping away tears I hadn't even realized I'd shed.

I manage a watery smile. "You know what? I'm hungry. You want to just cede my victory and let's go get some lunch?"

"You're clearly the victor," he says, standing and holding out a hand to help me up. "The victor gets to decide on lunch."

"Good," I say. "Then we're going to Sandy's. Burgers and fries and custard for dessert. It's the perfect meal to brighten a day. In case you're feeling a little blue at the way I just destroyed you on the golf course." I add the last with a smile, and am rewarded with his smile in return, full of understanding and appreciation for my not-so-subtle efforts to turn our mood around.

Sandy's is just a few blocks to the east on the same road. It's another Austin institution that's been around since the 40's. It has the look of a dive, and the food to match. And by that, I mean cheap and awesome.

It has a drive-through, but we park and stand in

the line at the window, then take our burgers and fries to the picnic tables in the back to chow down. This time, the conversation is lighter, with me waxing poetic about my hometown, especially this area that's so close to the river, which has always been one of my favorite places to spend a weekend.

"I'm getting to know this area pretty well," he says, pointing to his building on the other side of the river, which flows just about a block away. "But this place is a new find." He holds up the remnants of the burger he's wolfed down. "It's pretty life-changing."

"I know, right? Come on," I add, finishing my own food. "We need ice cream."

It's actually frozen custard, and we each get a cone, then eat it as we walk the relatively short distance to the river. We spend another hour on the path before returning to his car, which fortunately wasn't towed from Sandy's parking lot.

"I'll get you home," he says, as the afternoon winds down. "From what you've said, you have some writing to do."

I almost argue, but he's right. Besides, it's been a great day so far, despite—or maybe partly because of—the revelations about what happened during the years we were apart.

I navigate over surface streets so that he doesn't have to get back on MoPac, the North-South freeway that runs on the west side of town. Instead, we take South Lamar, and I point out some of my favorite places to shop and eat. Funky retail shops, consignment stores, bakeries, and, of course, Tex-Mex eateries.

When we reach my South Austin house just off Bro-die Lane, he walks me to the door.

"Thanks," I say, once I've unlocked the place and am standing on the threshold. "I honestly wasn't sure when I saw you on my porch, but this was fun."

"I'm glad you enjoyed it. It was a toss-up between Peter Pan or Hippie Hollow," he says, referring to the clothing optional park on the shores of Lake Travis.

"And you chose the golf," I say, raising my brows. Then I flash him a flirty grin, before dipping my gaze down toward his crotch. I'm playing with fire, I know, but I can't help myself. "Too bad for me."

"Well, it's November," he says, his voice deadpan. "I figured the chill wouldn't show off my assets."

I snort with laughter as he winks, then turns his back and walks to his car.

I go inside, smiling happily.

All in all, it was a really good day.

CHAPTER 13

"I FLIRTED WITH him," I tell Ares the next morning, as we sit on the back porch, sharing the Sunday paper. "I shouldn't have done that."

He glances at me over the comics page, which he habitually reads first before diving into the actual news. "Why not?"

"Why not?" I repeat, my voicing rising with incredulity. Because, hello. Most obvious thing in the universe. "Because we're not together. Because it's a bad idea. Because therein lies the path to madness."

He studies me for a minute, then folds the paper and puts it on the small wooden table that sits between us. "You're serious."

"Don't I sound serious?" But he just shakes his head, and I sigh. "We talked. We both acknowledged that things have changed. We're different people now. And the whole idea of spending some time together yesterday was to just get to know each other again."

"Right. Still not seeing the problem."

I take a sip of my coffee, then sigh loudly. "Never mind." Clearly, I'll have to deal with my angsty, post-date remorse by myself. I glance at my watch. Only eight.

Which means it's six in LA. Which means Celia will kill me if I call her for some BFF handholding.

"I'm going to get a fresh cup and a donut," I say. Donuts are Ares' Sunday morning vice, and being at my house isn't sufficient to change his routine. He actually got up this morning, jogged to the donut store a few blocks down on Brodie, then jogged back with a dozen warm, assorted donuts. I would call him out on the irony, but I'm afraid he'd banish me from Donutlandia.

I return with a fresh coffee and the entire box. I figure it's my duty to help him eat them, thus saving him from one of his vices.

"I thought you used to be so in love with this guy that the world stopped turning," Ares says, plucking a chocolate covered donut from the box.

I grab a glazed. "We were."

"Then why are you fighting it now?"

"I—"

I pause, the donut not quite to my mouth. *Because he'll hurt me. Because he'll leave. Because we don't even really know each other anymore.*

Because I'm scared.

A million familiar reasons rattle around in my head, and each one is real and true. But for some reason, after yesterday, none of them are quite as scary as they used to be.

But that's a problem, too. Because I need to be smart. I know what happens when you let your guard down, after all.

"Because we're working together," I finally say, then shove half the donut into my mouth so that he can't interrogate me anymore.

"Uh-huh." He manages to convey worlds of disbelief in just his tone. So much, that I regret stuffing my mouth.

"Es nofa goo dea," I say.

"Not a good idea?" he translates.

I nod and swallow. "Really not. We're going to be working close together on this one, and with the compressed time frame, we'll be working late hours, too."

"Interesting," he says, then reaches for another donut.

I frown. "What is?"

He's chewing, so he simply shrugs. And since he's not as uncouth as me, I have to wait for him to swallow.

"I didn't realize you had so little self-control," he says. "Or is Noah the one who doesn't have a handle on himself?"

"What are you talking about?"

"I'm just surprised to learn that you both have so little self-control that you're afraid you'll end up going at it like bunnies on the copy machine if you even suggest to each other that you're interested in *that* way."

"Ares…"

"Don't say my name that way."

"What way?"

"As if I'm being unreasonable or unfair."

I cross my arms and sit back in my chair. I know I'm being huffy, but I feel justified. "Fine. I'm listening."

"Look, all I'm saying is that you slept with the guy, right?"

"Yes, but—"

"And then you went out with him and had a good time."

I can hardly deny it.

"And you told me that you flirted with him, so in the—what?—thirty-six hours since you guys boinked like bunnies, you haven't lost interest. I mean, he still gets you hot."

"What is it with you and bunnies?"

He stares me down, and I sit back, my hands raised in surrender. "Yes. Still attracted." Understatement, much? That, however, I don't say out loud.

"And so I ask again, what's the problem?"

I try to think of what to say. Some magical words that will make Ares understand. Except he already understands—I know he does. He's known me all of my adult life. So I tell him the truth. "I don't think I can survive the hurt when he leaves again."

"How do you know he will?" His voice is gentle, and that makes it worse. Because he's being nice, and I just want to run from everything he's saying.

"Look," he continues, when I remain silent, "I get what you're afraid of. I do. And, yeah. Maybe you were dealt a shit hand. But your dad didn't leave you. He left your mom."

"Bullshit," I say. "He divorced my mom, sure. But I'm the one he left. Regular visits from the time I was four until I was seven, and then he remarries and I never see him again. Just Christmas and birthday cards, and even those stopped when Mom remarried. With my mother at least, he did it the way you're supposed to, with a judge and a court order and all that. With me, he just crept off into the shadows."

"You're right," Ares says. "I'm sorry. But he's the asshole. Don't let him paint your life."

I swallow. "Maybe so. But I seem to be a magnet for assholes. Look at Cameron's dad. And my mom, for that matter."

My mother remarried when I was nine, and Cam was born when I was ten. His father—my stepdad—left before Cam's first birthday, sneaking out in the middle of the night with only a note for my mother and not even a hug for me, even though he'd always been great to me before that. Taking me to parks, talking to me, promising me that he was my daddy now.

And then, poof, he was gone. Guess he was right; he was just like my daddy.

In my head, I know that he was a jerk, too. And I know that both he and my father left because of my mom, not me. She had her own problems, God knew. But they just walked. They didn't say goodbye. They were there—and then they weren't. And no matter how hard I tried to be rational and make sense of it, their abandonment scarred me.

Maybe with a different mother, I would have healed. One who poured on love. Or even one who was tough and assured me that we'd get through it—that what those men did wasn't a reflection on me.

But that wasn't my mom, not by a long shot. And when I was twelve and Cam was almost two, she took us to her mother's house in Austin, supposedly so that Grams would watch us while Mom had some adult time.

That was the last I ever saw of her, not counting five

Christmas cards—without return addresses—that came over the course of the next ten years. She didn't even come to Gram's funeral.

And, yeah, I know it's not my fault. And I know it's not Cam's fault. If anything, it's my mom's fault—she's the one who left, and considering everything, it's a fair bet that she's the reason the men left, too.

But it feels like it's me. And the scars are real. And even though I know the truth, my heart has never really healed.

I pull my feet up onto the seat of the chair and hug my knees, hating that I'm so vulnerable. And hating more that Ares sees it so clearly.

"And Owen?" Ares says gently.

I whip my head over, surprised. "What about him?"

"You're the one who left him."

I cringe, then put my feet down as I reach for my coffee. I take a sip, knowing that I'm stalling, then say, "That's just timing. He would have left me for that grad student."

"And you know that why? Because he slept with you?"

Owen Porter teaches at the business school, but I only had him for one introductory class, and we didn't start dating until much later. Things were fine while I was in school, but once I graduated and started pouring my energy into Crown Consulting, we started to drift apart. He even talked about taking a job at another college, even though he knew my business was rooted in Austin.

Honestly, I'm not sure we were that together in the

first place. But we got along, and there was genuine affection, and when we'd married, he'd seemed like a safe harbor.

When things started to get rocky, all I did was get a jump on the inevitable, and I tell Ares as much.

Even as I speak, though, I can't deny the little twist in my gut. Because maybe, deep down, *maybe* I knew that if I'd stuck, things would have gotten better. But I couldn't stay and take the risk. Leaving was hard enough on my heart. If he'd been the one to walk, I think it would have destroyed me.

"Look, Owen was never my favorite guy," Ares says, "but you imagined him hooking up with a grad student and packing his bags because of your issues. He never actually said or did anything, did he? Because if he did, you never told me or Cam."

I scowl, but I don't respond. He's right.

"I'm just saying, keep an open mind," he continues. "Because if you don't, you're going to end up alone. Or worse, Noah will end up with someone else."

I turn sharply to him, and Ares smiles knowingly.

"Yeah," he says, "that hurts because you care. So don't pretend like you don't. Most of all, don't fuck up, okay?"

CHAPTER 14

B ECAUSE I SPENT so much energy not thinking about Ares' words, I get a lot of writing done Sunday morning. It's barely past noon when I email the lyrics of two completely new songs to Celia, and am rewarded by her emoji-laden cyber-squeal of joy.

In the afternoon, I turn my attention to work, and dive into an in-depth, meticulous review of my plans for the rollout. I spend hours going over every point and turning my notes into a PowerPoint presentation. Overkill, maybe. But considering the time crunch, I want everybody on the team to be as much in my head as possible.

There are no calls or texts from Noah, and I tell myself I don't care. Because why would he call or text? Or email? Or stop by? We had a great time yesterday, but the day served its purpose, and tomorrow we can go to work and not feel awkward around each other.

Still, I can't help wondering what he's doing today. Or, more accurately, I can't help wondering who he's doing it with.

Frustrated by the direction of my own thoughts, I force my attention back to work. On the dual campaigns for the trade and for consumers. On the presentation team I want to form, so that companies that may be on the fence about the viability of the project can see it in action. Of the television and web ads I want to get in place for the commercial market. And, most of all, the drip campaign counting down to the product's release.

I'm at the Stark offices by seven, and the receptionist leads me to the conference room that is going to be our ground zero. Maia's already there, her laptop open and her fingers flying over the keyboard. Her hair is pulled back from her face in dozens of neat cornrows that fall down her back, each fastened with a brightly colored bead.

She wears neon purple glasses that stand out against her ebony skin, and she's glancing between the papers at her elbow and the screen as she types. Documents are stacked neatly in front of every chair, and the projector is already on as she runs through the presentation I emailed her late last night.

She tilts her head as she pulls down her computer glasses, then looks over the frames and smiles at me. "Morning. I think we're all set."

"And that's why I adore you," I say. Maia's worked with me for a while now, and since I realized I'd do pretty much anything to keep her, I offered her a partnership a few months ago, which she eagerly accepted. She's six years younger than me, and I hired her while she was still working toward her MBA, then covered her last semester's tuition because I wanted her on my team. She's ridiculously hard-working and has some of the most original ideas I've ever heard.

She's also ambitious and as keen as I am at building Crown Consulting into a kick ass operation. Plus, she's no dummy, and she knows that her partnership coupled with me doubling up on my music career, means her trajectory here is pretty much a straight path to the top.

Most important, though, we work well together, she's got a wicked sense of humor, and we share a secret love of bad reality television and peanut butter M&Ms.

"Mr. Carter assigned all the offices on this hall to your team," the receptionist says to both of us. "I took the liberty of selecting the corner offices for the two of you," she adds. "Your name plates are on the doors. I'm Elise, by the way. Let me know if you need any help getting settled. You're expecting five more for this morning's meeting?"

"From our team," Maia says, standing up to hand Elise a list of names. "And then the in-house folks?" She says the last as a question, looking at me.

"Our people at eight," I say. "Noah and the Stark marketing people at ten. That gives us two hours to make sure our team is up to speed and the plan is perfect. Once the Stark folks are in the room, I want to hit the ground running. With the truncated time frame, we don't have the luxury of wasting minutes."

"Right-o," Maia says, as I turn back to Elise.

"Thanks again, and just send everyone this way when they arrive."

Elise promises to do that, and Maia and I dive into work, with me pulling a chair over so that I can see her screen as we make final tweaks on the presentation.

We've been going at it for over half an hour when

there's a light tap at the door. I look up, see Noah, and my heart skitters in my chest.

At my interview, I'd been too nervous to pay attention to what he'd been wearing. Now, though…

Well, now, all I can think is *wow*.

He's in a gray pinstriped suit with a shirt of such pale blue it's almost silver. His tie, a dark blue with gunmetal gray stripes, accentuates the outfit, which was clearly tailored, not to mention expensive.

But it's not the suit, but the way Noah wears it that has my mouth going dry. This is a Noah I've only seen hints of; this is the Noah who runs this entire operation. And if the look of confidence on his face is any indication, he does it exceptionally well.

"Good morning," he says, his eyes lingering on me for a second too long before he turns his attention to Maia. "I'm Noah Carter," he says, walking toward her and extending his hand. "You must be Maia Hancock."

"Nice to meet you," Maia says. "We weren't expecting you until ten, but if you want us to run you through it now, we're ready."

"I have no doubt. But actually, I need to talk to you," he says, turning toward me. A ball of irritation forms in my stomach, and I force myself to manage a civil smile.

"Sure. Let's step outside." I start that direction, barely noticing the way his brow furrows as I pass him. He's right behind me, and I shut the door. Then, for good measure, I drag him into the empty office across the hall. I want privacy before I lay into him.

"What the hell are you doing?" I say, my voice low, but tight. Even with the door closed, we could be overheard. "The last thing I want is for folks to know that there's something going on with us." I've already told Maia we have a history, but I also told her that it was all very much in the past.

His brows rise, and he looks like he's about to laugh. Which, of course, only makes me more annoyed.

"What am I doing? I was introducing myself to your colleague. Who, according to the resume on your website, seems extremely competent. What makes you think I was doing anything more?"

"You smiled at me," I say, and the moment the words are out of my mouth, I regret them. Clearly, I'm an idiot.

"I'll make sure not to do that again," he says dryly.

"And you said you needed to talk to me. Alone. Why would you need to do that?"

"I didn't," he says. "You assumed it." He takes a step closer, and I wish he'd back up. He's making it even harder to think straight.

"But since we're here," he says, "I'll say that I enjoyed Saturday very much. And it took a lot of willpower not to call you yesterday and invite you out for a walk around the lake."

"Oh. Well. I was working." My voice is level, but I fight to hide the surprising little twinge of disappointment that I'd missed out on seeing him. I quash it down. "What did you need to talk about this morning?"

"I'm going to tell the whole team, but I wanted to give you a heads up about possible corporate espionage."

"Great," I say ironically after he tells me the details of his conversation with Mr. Stark. "Hopefully, we're not a target, and it's just limited to the Israeli company we're racing to the finish line."

"Fingers crossed," he says as we head back to the conference room. He fills Maia in, who looks at me suspiciously the entire time he's talking. To the point that I rub my hand over my mouth in case I have cream cheese on my chin. Noah and I had returned to find a full spread, and I'd dug in immediately.

But, no. My chin is clean. And I can't help but wonder what my perceptive soon-to-be partner is seeing that I'm not.

We've just finished bringing Noah up to speed when my team arrives, a group of five freelancers that I've used on various projects. I trust them all, and I'm also certain that Noah has vetted them, in light of the espionage concerns. So now I trust them even more. After quick meetings with each of them in turn, it's time for the Stark marketing team to join us.

Soon the conference room is full, and the presentation begins.

Noah starts by discussing the espionage concerns, which I think is a brilliant move, as it underscores his trust in his team, something that's especially key since he's new to the company.

After that, he turns the meeting over to me. I gather the slippery stack of file folders, head to the front of the table, and then drop everything when I'm just inches from Noah.

Stellar.

I crouch immediately, trying to gather the loose sheets, my cheeks burning because I'm certain that Noah has a rather undignified view of my ass pressed tight against my linen skirt as I crawl halfway under the table.

Then he's down on all fours beside me. "Fancy meeting you here," he says, and I laugh.

"I like to command control of a room," I say.

"You got everyone's attention, all right."

I scowl at him, but he just laughs, then passes me a sheath of papers. For a moment, his fingers linger on mine, then our eyes meet. One second, then another, and it's as if I can feel the tension running all the way through me, electrifying my skin. Making me hyperaware of even the air around me.

I open my mouth, but I have no idea what I'm going to say. That's okay, though. Noah says it for me.

"Go on. Show everyone what you've got."

He helps me up, and that's exactly what I do. My clumsiness is a tiny blip in a sea of productivity. We go through the plan, assign goals and tasks, and make sure the timeline is clear. I handle questions, give Maia the floor so that the team knows they can go to her as well, and then sit back in my chair as we move on to the final point of today's meeting.

"Product name," I say, then nod to Maia who puts up the slide. "We propose Red Brick for a number of reasons. It has both corporate and commercial appeal. It suggests strength, but also has an element of both danger and protection. You can hurt someone with a brick—but you can also build. Red has similar connotations. We're marketing a product that has intense security applications, but that is a bit edgy and potentially controversial. And also very, very useful for law enforcement. Red for danger. Red for life. Red for help and assistance and protection. Just think of the Red Cross, right?"

We toss that around for a while, but ultimately, the name is approved unanimously, although only Noah's vote truly counts. We move from there to the drip campaign I want to get started next week—a slow build to introduce the product to our core markets.

And then, right in time for a late lunch, we finally break.

"I think that went great," Maia says, after Noah and his group have left. "You all had great suggestions," she tells the team, then dismisses them to go work on their assigned tasks. "God, I love the power," she says to me, and I burst out laughing.

"Don't make me have to take it back," I say, teasing. She's accepted my offer of partnership, but we're still waiting for my lawyer to get back with the various bits of paperwork.

"You'd never," she says. "You love me too much, and that went too smoothly."

"It did," I agree, pleased. "I'm going to go find this office that Elise assigned me and see if I can narrow down a list of possible companies for testimonials." One thing we're planning to do is offer early releases of Red Brick to potential clients for beta-testing and marketing testimonials.

Right now, though, we don't have those beta-testers in place.

I'm mentally running down a list of companies as I step into my office, only to stop dead when I find Noah leaning against the edge of my desk.

"Great meeting," he says.

"Thanks." I've done hundreds of rollouts, but this is the first time a client's praise has made me feel quite so warm and wonderful.

Deliberately, I move behind the desk and take a seat in my new chair. "Nice," I say. "Most clients just shove us in a conference room."

"Maybe I wanted you to have privacy," he says, going to shut the door.

"Noah." My voice is soft. Breathy. But it's also firm.

He shakes his head. "So that you can get work done," he says, and I feel my cheeks heat all over again.

"You're playing with me on purpose, aren't you?"

"Never," he says, but I have to press my lips together to keep from laughing. He is, of course. And the smile that is now crinkling at the corners of his eyes proves it.

"Actually," he continues, taking a seat opposite me. "The privacy does come in handy. I wanted to tell you that I have a couple of ideas for security companies we can talk to about beta-testing. A good friend heads up Sykes Security and has access to WORR."

"Which is?"

"The World Organization for Rescue and Rehabilitation. It's a private organization that works closely with international law enforcement."

"Which you know about from when you were doing the covert work?"

"Right," he says. "Which is another reason the door is closed."

I realize just how much he told me during our afternoon out. Personal things. Private things. And several things that weren't his to tell. "Thanks," I say.

"For what?"

"For trusting me."

"I do," he says, and for a moment silence hangs between us. Then he clears his throat and adds, "We can't actually use Stark International's security team to beta our own product, but I'm sure that Ryan Hunter—he heads it up—will have some additional suggestions."

"This is all great. Can you make the introductions and I'll call them?"

"Absolutely. In fact, I can introduce you to Ryan next week when we go to LA."

I lean back in my chair, my fingers twined behind my head. "We're going to Los Angeles?"

"The wrap party for *M. Sterious* is next Thursday."

"That superhero movie?" I'm incredibly confused.

"My friend Lyle's the lead guy," he explains. "And you're coming to the party. As my plus one."

I sit up, the chair spring bouncing me back faster than I had expected. "Noah!"

"As a friend and a business colleague only."

"No," I say firmly. "I have too much to do here. And—"

"And what?"

I have a killer glare when I need to, and now I aim it hard at him. "There's just too much work and too little time."

He says nothing, and after a while I can't hold the glare any longer. I look down at the desktop and try to calm down.

When I look back up, I find his eyes on me, like I'm

some complicated equation. Which, I suppose I am. He's invited me for business. I'm not going because it feels personal.

But it only feels that way because I'm seeing him that way. And because I do have feelings for him.

And because, more than anything, I want to protect my heart.

"You're right," he finally says, his voice firmly professional. "I'll speak to them, and if they're interested we can get on a call. That will be fine."

He's right, that will be fine. Better, even.

I nod in agreement, trying to ignore the knot in my stomach that keeps twisting and turning and tightening.

"Great," I say briskly. "Now, I have some rough sketches for the print ads I want you to look at…"

FOR THE REST of the week, Maia and I knuckle down with the team. Noah, too, though of course he has an entire company to run simultaneous to us planning the Red Brick rollout.

Even so, he's in the trenches daily, working shoulder to shoulder with me, and when I point out that he has other responsibilities, he reminds me that while Stark Applied Technology is firmly established, the Austin office is still new—and still proving itself. Red Brick is its first high profile product.

As if there weren't enough pressure.

I'd thought that his daily presence would be awkward; I was wrong. Just the opposite, actually. The days fly by and we fall into a rhythm. A pattern. I work closely with him, and it's wonderful. We instinctively know what the other wants. Needs. Honestly, if it were sex, it would be the best ever.

I know I shouldn't be thinking like that. But as the days pass—as I watch him competently sketch changes to a design or authoritatively tell the team in which direction to move—I find myself inching closer to something I know I should be backing away from.

And when he's standing behind me, his hand pressed to my shoulder as we look at the laptop screen, it's everything I can do to think about the words and images in front of us, and not the pressure of his touch. Or the way he could so easily slide his hand down to caress my breast, or twine his fingers in my hair and force my head back for a long, deep kiss.

Honestly, I think I've used my vibrator more in the past week than all of last year. It's a good thing Ares has already left on tour and I have the house to myself. I'd be mortified if he heard me all alone in my room.

And the vivid dreams in which Noah has a starring role… Oh. My.

Between my sleepless nights and my long hours at work, I'm bordering on exhausted. But at the same time, I've never been more pumped up. The campaign prep is going great, and every day the thought of seeing Noah again is as invigorating as coffee.

Well, not quite. I'm drinking so much coffee I should probably hook myself to an IV.

"You're really good at this," Noah says, as he and I are bent over some mock-ups that the art department sent up to the conference room.

"Thanks." I smile up at him, feeling more pleased by his praise than I should. After all, he hired me, didn't he? Of course, he thinks I'm competent.

He's smiling back at me, his eyes crinkling at the corner, his hair wild from having run his fingers through it at least a dozen times that morning. He looks like he just rolled out of bed, and my heart does a little flip-flop.

I quickly turn back to the mock-ups so that he can't look in my eyes and see my thoughts. "I like the challenge," I continue, mostly to fill the silence. "So much that I sometimes think I shouldn't even consider starting Pink Chameleon up again."

"Why?" He steps back from the table.

I turn to see him better. "I don't know," I say, as Maia steps into the room and heads to the far side of the conference table where her laptop is set up.

I glance at her, but she's already tapping the keyboard, obviously deep into some project of her own.

I turn back to Noah, who's clearly waiting for a better response from me. "I guess I think about what a good thing I have with Crown Consulting. Why would I want to risk that?" Not that I would be. Maia has the skill to keep the business alive. I frown, trying to order my thoughts. "Or, I guess, why do I need more?"

"Fair enough," he says. "But you're talented and you're passionate and you're ambitious. Don't settle just because that's comfortable. You should go after what you want."

I swallow, hearing the words in a different context. Not music, but *him*.

I look away. "I guess. I don't know."

"Or maybe that's not really why you're hesitating."

"What?" There's a ridiculous note of panic in my voice, and I want to kick myself.

"I just wonder if maybe you're afraid of making it. Because you came so close one time, and then it all got ripped away."

I gape at him, and it takes me a moment to realize he's still talking about singing and not us. "I…"

I trail off. I have no idea what to say.

His smile is gentle. "Sorry. I didn't mean to sound preachy. All I wanted to say was that I think you have the talent to make it. Don't deny yourself just because you're scared and comfortable with the status quo. You'll only regret it."

"Thanks," I say, his belief in my talent meaning more to me than it should.

"Anytime." This time his grin is wide, even a little playful. He heads toward the door. "I'm due on a conference call. I'll check in later."

I nod, then stare stupidly at the closed door once he's gone.

"*What* is with you two?" Maia demands, the second I turn around.

"What? Nothing." I look down at the mock-ups. "We're just friends, that's all." I've told her about our past, but only the short version. Dated years ago. Broke up. Now working together.

"Yeah. Sure."

"Are you ready to go over the national media budget?"

J. KENNER

"Absolutely," she says, but I can tell from the tone of her voice that this conversation isn't over. We've become too close in the last few years for her to let this drop.

Maybe that's good. Maybe I need someone to talk to. Because right now, I think I'm a danger to myself.

Because the biggest thought in my mind at this very moment, is that not jumping all over his suggestion that we be Friends With Benefits was a really, *really* stupid move.

CHAPTER 15

FOR HIS ENTIRE career, Noah had been someone who habitually got to work early. Now, faced with the knowledge that each morning he'd see Kiki, he found himself arriving not just early, but ridiculously, obscenely, obsessively early.

It was worth it, though.

He liked walking down to the twenty-second floor from his office on twenty-three and catching her at her desk before eight. For the first couple of days, he'd come armed with a question about work. Then he gave that up. The truth was, he just wanted to see her. Chat with her. About the job, about work. About whatever was on their minds.

And even though she didn't say it, he knew she looked forward to their quiet mornings, too. He'd suspected as much when she offered him a croissant, saying that the bakery had messed up her order.

The next time, he was certain she'd intentionally brought him a muffin, but he pretended to believe her bullshit bakery error story.

The third time, neither of them pretended, and they sat together on the small sofa in her office, drank coffee and ate cheese Danish. They'd fallen into a pattern. Coffee and baked goods while they chatted about nothing in particular. Then, after about fifteen minutes of that, they'd shift seamlessly into work mode.

It wasn't his usual way to dive into the day, but damned if he wasn't getting used to it.

Fridays were always crazy, and this one was no exception. He'd gotten a call from a European vendor, and now he was late getting out the door. In the past, he wouldn't have cared, but now the thought of skipping his morning Kiki-time edged him toward a foul mood.

Hurrying, he crossed the condo lobby, then pushed open the glass doors. He started to veer right toward Congress, then stopped cold when he saw that same damn green truck parked across the street. And once again there was someone in the driver's seat, slumped down and wearing a ball cap.

Maybe it was nothing.

Maybe it was none of his business.

But maybe it was a corporate spy, and Noah intended to find out.

He checked himself, and instead of going right, he headed straight across the narrow driveway that ran in front of the condo. He hit the sidewalk, and then—even though he was in the middle of the block without a crosswalk and traffic was heavy—he started across the one-way street, determined to see just who the hell was in that truck.

He didn't make it.

The driver turned, the truck started, and right as Noah hit the middle of the street, the damn thing pulled out away from the curb.

This time, he had the presence of mind to check the license plate—and when he saw that there wasn't one, he spat out a curse as he continued walking to work.

The moment he stepped into her office, Kiki rose to her feet, her eyes skimming over him with concern. "Are you okay?"

And there it was—that sweet little kick in his gut. The way she surprised him by the simple fact that she knew him. It was the reason why being around her was both hard—and the easiest thing in the world.

"Fine," he said. "Just baffled and a little concerned." He took a seat, then told her about the green truck.

She passed him a blueberry muffin and sat on the couch beside him. "Do you think it has to do with Red Brick? What Mr. Stark told you about espionage?"

He hadn't realized how much he'd feared looking paranoid until she spoke, and her words confirmed he wasn't overreacting. "I don't know, but if I see it again, I'll let Stark know."

She nodded approval. "Good. Oh, and check this out." She got up and went to her desk, practically dancing her way back to hand him the most recent copy of *X-Tech*, a prestigious trade publication that focused on tech and security. He knew the team had been targeting them to run a feature on Red Brick, and the way she was doing a combination happy dance and victory march, told him they'd gotten the interview.

Even better, it made him laugh.

"Don't you dare tease me," she said, circling her desk as she did a couple of fist pumps. "I worked my ass off lining that up." She danced her way back to him again, and this time, he grabbed her hand and tugged her down to the couch.

"Spoilsport," she teased, but she was smiling. And she hadn't let go of his hand.

She met his eyes, and he heard her sharp, shuddering breath before she gently tugged her hand away, then reached for her coffee and held her mug in both hands, as if she wanted to stop herself from reaching for him again.

"I'm going to a housewarming party on Sunday," he said, the words coming unplanned. "You should join me."

"I should? Why's that?"

She wasn't looking at him, but he could hear the tease in her voice. But he wasn't teasing when he answered. "Because I want you to."

She turned to him, her eyes wide with surprise, her freckles showing up a little more against her flushed cheeks. "Oh." She licked her lips, and it wasn't until the slow smile spread across her face that he realized he'd been holding his breath. "In that case, I'd love to."

"ARES GREW UP in this neighborhood," Kiki said Sunday as they drove north on Chicon Street in East

Austin. "I came with him a few times in college to see his parents. It's changed a lot. They lived over that way, by the cemetery." She pointed vaguely to the left, back toward downtown. "We used to walk through it and have long talks about the meaning of life."

Noah hadn't grown up in Austin, but he was familiar with the city's efforts to revitalize the historically lower income area east of the Interstate. Over a decade ago, a lot of young professionals had started buying up the houses to either tear down or renovate, and as the smaller bungalows were replaced with modern, urban dwellings, more businesses moved in to service the newer, moneyed residents. The problem, of course, was that the long-time residents ended up priced out of their homes, unable to afford the increase in property taxes that came with the new, shinier East Austin.

"It's hard," Kiki agreed when he said as much. "After Ares' father died, his mom couldn't afford the taxes. She sold it for a decent amount, but not enough to buy another place in Austin. She's renting now in Dallas near his sister." She shrugged. "But there are upsides, too. The restaurants, the cleanup. Crime is down. But it makes me sad that people who lived here for generations can't hang onto their homes."

She sighed wistfully. "Ares was just starting to perform when we were in college, and he'd sing for his cousins at his house. I'd come along and sing backup or whatever he needed. And his mom would stuff us full of tamales. It was heaven."

"The tamales or the singing?" he asked, as his car's navigation system ordered him to make a left.

"Both. But mostly the singing."

He made the turn, then took his eyes off the road long enough to note the way she was still smiling at the memory. "I was thinking about what you said the other day," he said. "About you considering backing off from Pink Chameleon."

"You think I should," she guessed. "I have a good thing going with Crown Consulting, and I need to be a grown-up about my life and career."

"Actually, I was going to say that you need to go for it. You've always wanted to sing, and you should grab what you want when you can."

It struck him that he wasn't following his own advice. He wanted Kiki, but he sure as hell hadn't grabbed her.

Except that wasn't the same at all. He was keeping his distance because that's what she wanted. He was respecting her boundaries.

But maybe now it was time to start chipping away...

"It's scary," she said, her words unintentionally tracking his thoughts. "I'm so much older now, and I don't know if our music is even relevant, and touring doesn't sound nearly as cool as it used to. But at the same time, I want to sing. I want to perform. And I don't want to wake up and be angry with myself for not trying."

"Which is exactly what I just said."

She laughed. "Yeah. I guess it is. You know, this is the second time you've encouraged me to dive into Pink Chameleon."

"I was just a sounding board the other day," he protested.

"No, I mean now, and back when we lived in Los Angeles."

"Oh." He forced his body to relax. "Sorry if I brought up bad memories."

"No," she said quickly, then gently touched his arm. "No, I didn't mean it that way. Actually, I like it. It's nice having someone watch my back again. Gives me a reality check."

"What are friends for?" he asked as the car announced that they'd arrived at their destination, a pale blue bungalow that was probably built in the thirties, and looked as if it had been recently refurbished.

He found a spot on the street and killed the engine. He was about to open his door and get out when Kiki put her hand on his arm again. "I'm glad," she said. "That you're here. That we're friends again." Her smile was sweet, maybe even a little shy. "Working with you.... It's been great. I've missed ... well, I missed it."

"So have I," he said, his throat suddenly dry. "And I'm glad we're friends again, too."

And he was. Genuinely, honestly happy.

But that didn't mean that he didn't want more.

They got out of the car and followed the yard sign that told them to come in through the back gate.

They followed a crushed granite path to a xeriscaped backyard where a dozen or so people mingled—including a tall, slender blonde. *Evie.*

She was chatting with Griffin, their host, but for a second, she looked away from Griffin and straight at Noah. Their eyes met. Then her gaze flickered to Kiki and quickly back to Noah. She flashed a knowing smile, then returned her attention to Griffin.

Beside Noah, Kiki was scanning the party, apparently oblivious. "Who's the host?"

"That's him," Noah said, pointing.

"We should go say hi."

Since he wasn't at all interested in talking with Evie, he was about to suggest they get a drink first. But he didn't have to use that ploy, as he was rescued by Wyatt and Kelsey, who came up and introduced themselves.

"I saw *A Woman in Mind* in Dallas," Kiki said. "It was spectacular."

"I'm glad you enjoyed it," Wyatt said.

"So much. And I saw the prints in Noah's apartment. They're exceptional."

"Oh?" Kelsey asked innocently. Too innocently, Noah thought. "The ones on the wall near his bed? So, are you two dating? I'm allowed to be nosy because the host's my brother. Plus, Noah's told us about you, and I've had my fingers crossed."

"Kelsey," Wyatt chastised, but Noah was pleased to see that Kiki only laughed.

"We're just friends," she said, but her tone was almost like a question, and that little bit of inflection gave him hope.

"And colleagues," he added, though the second the words escaped him, he wanted to call them back. Tossing work up felt like a wall. And he didn't want any more walls.

He was considering what else he could say when he heard a female squeal, and a dark-haired girl in leggings and an oversized loose knit sweater bounded over, calling Kiki's name.

"Mina?" Kiki asked, then held out her arms as the younger woman embraced her. "What on earth are you doing here?"

"I'm interning for Griffin," she said, as Kiki turned her toward Noah. "Mina is Cam's best friend's sister. I used to babysit her. It is *so* awesome to see you."

Noah and Mina did the introduction thing, and then she and Kiki wandered off together, clearly following the path down memory lane.

Wyatt had stepped away to talk to someone else, but Kelsey had lingered. Now, she edged Noah aside, her arms crossed and her expression stern. "Colleagues?" she said. "Seriously? You like this girl and that's the best you can do?"

"I know. Lame."

"But recoverable," she said boldly, as if she were a relationship general leading the charge. "So how is it really going with you two?"

He tried to think how to explain it to her. "She's right—we are friends. But—"

"But you haven't gotten past the speed bump to move on to anything more?"

"That's not a bad way of putting it." He dragged his fingers through his hair. It wasn't just her desire to stay at arms-length that was stymieing them. It was their past. The memory of pain. And what he wanted—no, what he needed—to do was tell her flat out that he wanted more. That he knew he'd hurt her and wanted to spend the rest of his life making it up to her.

"That," Kelsey said softly.

Noah frowned, confused. "What?"

"Whatever you were thinking that gave you such a wistful look. Just go tell her that."

"Easier said than done."

She gave him a gentle shove. "Sure it is ... if you never do it." She cut a glance toward Kiki, who was laughing as Mina bounced away. "See? She's free. So, *go*."

So he went. And, what the hell. Maybe it was time.

"Hey," he said, moving to her side, his heart flipping a bit when she flashed that sweet smile before turning her attention back to the guests, her eyes skimming as if looking for someone.

He put a hand on her arm. "I thought we could run inside and get a drink."

"Sure." She tilted her head toward him. "Can you believe Mina's here? She said Cam is, too, but I haven't seen him."

"Cam? Your brother?"

"Yeah, I know. Small world, right. But he's—oh! Cam!"

She lifted her free hand and waved, and a familiar twenty-something with dark-brown hair and an earring hurried over.

"Wait. That's Cam? The bartender at The Fix is your brother?"

She nodded as Cam scooped her into a hug. Not that her acknowledgment was necessary. Now that Noah knew, he could see the child from Kiki's old photos in the face of the man Cam had become.

Noah realized he should have connected the name of Cam-the-bartender with Cam-the-brother-who-interrupted in the alley. But he cut himself some slack. He'd been more than a little distracted that night.

"Why are you here?" Kiki asked him.

"Griff told Mina she could bring a guest, and her boyfriend's out of town. I'm a huge fan of Griff's show, so she thought I'd get a kick out of it, and invited me."

"I'm so glad. You might as well have moved to Dallas when you took that apartment by campus. I hardly see you anymore."

"Gee, *Mom*."

She rolled her eyes, though Noah knew that Cam was only half teasing. Long ago, Kiki had told Noah about their mother's abandonment and how she ended up being half-parent, half-sibling, especially after their grandmother's death.

"Listen," she said, "you two never actually met, but I talked about you both all the time. Cam, this is Noah. Noah, my brother Cam."

Noah felt the chill the instant Cam turned to face him with a bland, "Hey."

"We're working together," Kiki explained, apparently not feeling the frost.

"Hmm," Cam said. "Listen, there's something I've been meaning to call you about. I know it's a party and all, but can I borrow you for a sec? It's kind of important."

Immediately, concern flooded her face. "Of course." She reached for Noah and gave his hand a quick squeeze. "I'll find you in a bit."

"Sure," he said, wishing he could grab the hem of her shirt and pull her back to him. Because as much as he hoped that Cam was telling Kiki that she was an idiot for not throwing herself into Noah's arms, workplace romance be damned, that probably wasn't the case. After all, Cam had watched from half a continent away as Noah and Kiki had fallen in love … and as Noah had walked away.

No way was Cam telling his sister to give Noah a break. More likely, he was telling her to run for the hills.

And considering all the baggage that Noah now carried, maybe her brother was right.

CHAPTER 16

"NOAH?" CAM SAYS, sounding much older than his almost twenty-three years. "Seriously? You're back with Noah after what that bastard did to you?"

"I'm not back with him," I say, but already I'm lying to my little brother, because the truth is that I want to be back with him. Or, at least, I want to try.

Or I think I do.

Honestly, I'm so damn confused it's a wonder I can even think straight. Noah's gotten inside me again, and while it's a nice feeling, it's also a scary one.

Cam leans against the doorframe leading to Griffin's kitchen and stares me down.

"We're just friends, okay?" I say.

"But you want more."

Shit. When did my little brother get so perceptive?

"Maybe," I confess, then exhale noisily. "Honestly, all I know is it feels right being around him."

"Sure, until he rips your heart out again."

"He was young, and Darla was pregnant, and—"

"And you got screwed."

"I did," I say, my heart aching with the words and the memory. "But we're both older now, and we're not moving fast." For that matter, we're barely moving at all. But maybe that's good. I want to be friends. I want to trust him, to know him.

I want all that—and yet I crave so much more, and it's becoming hard to stay away. To play by the rules we set.

From the look on Cam's face, I think he's going to try to smack me down again, but Noah walks up to us, and I'm not sure if I'm relieved or fearful of imminent fisticuffs.

"Hey," he says, with a soft smile aimed right at my heart.

"Hey, back," I reply, unable to suppress my answering grin even though I know Cam is about to nosedive into a giant barrel of worry.

"I told Griffin I'd find you and introduce you," Noah says. "You'll like him. Just don't start listening to his podcast—at least not until after Red Brick is on the market. It's addictive."

"You know Griff?" Cam asks.

Noah nods. "I'm friends with Wyatt and Kelsey. I met him in LA before we both moved here. If it's any consolation, they all know me pretty well, and none of them think I'm the devil. Ask them if you want."

Cam's eyes widen, and my mouth drops open. "What are you—" I begin, but Noah cuts me off.

"We never met in person," he says to Cam, "so we don't know each other that well. Or at all, really. And I get that you're worried about your sister. But I want you to know that I thought I was doing the right thing all those years ago, I really did. I know it hurt Kiki, though, and I would give anything if I could heal that wound. I can't. All I can do is promise you that I'm not going to hurt her again."

He holds his hands out to his sides in a gesture of supplication. "That's it, Cameron. That's the best I can do. But I think Kiki's willing to give me a chance. I hope you do, too."

I feel a tightness in my chest and realize I've been holding my breath, awed by this unexpected speech ... and fearful of Cam's reaction.

My brother steps forward, and for the first time, I notice that they're almost the same height, with Noah having only a couple of inches on my brother. "If you hurt her," Cam says in a low, menacing voice I don't recognize, "I swear I will rearrange your face."

I almost laugh at the idea of my skinny little brother beating up a man like Noah, tall and lean, with a surfer's strength and the fierce determination of a man who doesn't step away from a battle.

But then my vision clears, and I truly see Cam for what may be the very first time. He's in the doorway, his shoulders wide, his chest filled out. His arms are ripped under the T-shirt he wears, and he looks young and strong and fierce. How had I not seen this before? My little brother's all grown up, and in the kind of way that makes me certain he could make good on his threat.

"Fair enough," Noah says, the holds out his hand. Cam hesitates, then takes it, and I fight the urge to squeal with delight. I have no idea what this means for me and Noah, but I know enough to be certain it's on the shiny side of good.

I aim a smirk at each of them in turn. "If you guys are done measuring your manliness, I'm going to go get a drink." I push past Cam into the kitchen. "Play nice, boys," I say, then pour myself a wine and exit out the back door, enjoying the fresh air and diminished testosterone.

I've stepped out onto a concrete stoop. There's a path that leads from this side area into the backyard proper, and I start to head that way, but I'm stopped by the pretty blonde woman I'd noticed when we first arrived. She's scowling at her phone and shoving it deep into her purse.

"Idiots," she says to me. "And they can't hold onto their idiocy until Monday and normal office hours. Honestly, you'd think I was working a death penalty case."

"You're a lawyer?"

"Entertainment," she says. "I'm Evie. I represent Griff, and since I was in town, he invited me. Well, my firm represents him. Bender, Twain & McGuire."

I shake my head, clueless.

"We're mostly in LA, but I met Griffin through Lyle Tarpin—who we also represent. And so I've started bouncing back and forth between LA and Texas." She shakes her head. "Sorry. When I drink, I ramble. And I've been drinking since I got here. It's shaping up to be a very long weekend."

I laugh, deciding that I like this woman.

"Do you know Lyle?" she asks. "Turns out a lot of the guests do. I'm almost surprised he didn't come here for the party."

"I only know his movies."

"He's a nice guy. Surprisingly down to earth. Some stars aren't, believe me. But we've become friendly, and I genuinely like his girlfriend. In fact, Lyle's the one who set me up with this guy I saw here earlier—Noah Carter. I should probably find him again and say hi." She shrugs. "Then again, I got the feeling he does the blind date thing a lot, so he probably doesn't care if I acknowledge him or not."

An unpleasant chill creeps up my spine. "You went out with Noah?"

"Blind date," she clarifies. Then she tilts her head as she studies my face. "Oh, hell," she says. "I saw you with him earlier, didn't I?"

"Yup. To be honest, he didn't mention you to me at all. Are you guys—I mean, have you…"

I have no idea what I want to ask, but fortunately Evie steps in to save me. "Oh, no, no. Just drinks. Nothing happened. In fact, he's the one who turned me down."

I glance over her, this extremely pretty, very well put together blonde. Honestly, I find that hard to believe.

"Truly," she says. "I was a little ticked off. I don't get snubbed that often."

I believe her.

But I'm still jealous. And for every Evie where nothing happened, how many women were there that he did sleep with?

It's a few minutes before I find Noah, and when I do, he's with Wyatt in the living room looking at some portraits of Griff and Kelsey that Wyatt shot for the two of them.

"There you are," Noah says, his expression brightening as I approach.

"Can we talk?" Neither my voice nor my expression is bright.

He glances to Wyatt, who moves a hand in what must be Guy Code for *she's your problem, not mine.*

"What's up?" Noah asks as he leads me back to the kitchen, which is empty at the moment, most of the alcohol having been moved to a table in the yard.

"I met Evie. She seems nice."

"The lawyer," he says. "She was." His brow furrows. "So?"

"I got the impression she was one in a string."

He'd been reaching for a plate of cheese and salami, but stops, his hand extended, as he looks at me. "Are you standing here—right now—and telling me that who I date—who I sleep with—is any of your business?"

His voice is gentle, but the words hit me with the force of a brick.

"Oh." It's the only word I can manage, and I realize that it's not him the spotlight is on, but me.

I draw a breath, gathering my courage. "Yes," I say firmly. "I am."

At first, I see no reaction. Then there's a flicker in his eyes. A spark of pleasure, happiness. Maybe heat. I'm not sure.

But I do know that my confession has moved him.

"I didn't sleep with Evie," he says.

"I see. And before. Was there a string?"

This time when he looks at me, his eyes are hard.

"Yes. But the last one was a long time before Evie. At least a month. And since Evie, there've been none."

I press my lips together. "There was me."

"*No.*" The word is fast and fierce. He moves closer, so he's standing right in front of me, and it's all I can do not to reach out and touch him. "You're something different."

"What?" I whisper, but he doesn't answer. Instead we're interrupted by a girl I don't recognize who stumbles into the kitchen, looks around, and shouts, "Damn. No wine."

"Come on," Noah says as soon as she's left. He holds out his hand out for me. "You haven't met Griffin yet, and we need to get going soon."

"We do?" I put my hand in his, shocked that after the undercurrent of revelations that have passed between us he doesn't yank me toward him. He doesn't wrap me in an embrace.

But his grip is warm, and it feels safe and comfortable. I squeeze his fingers, acknowledging this connection.

"There's someplace I want you to see," he continues. "And we need to be there by seven."

"Oh. Where?"

But he just smiles and leads me toward the door.

It's dark in the yard, but Griffin has a canopy of white lights on strings, making the area look like a fairyland. We find him on a stone bench, and the first thing I notice is his face. Noah had told me on the short walk that Griff was a survivor of a terrible gasoline fire when he was a kid, and that the right side of his body is seriously scarred.

He's wearing a hoodie, but even so, the scars are visible, and my heart aches for the little boy he'd been, and the physical and emotional pain he must have suffered.

Then he speaks, and his voice is so beautiful and rich, I almost forget the scars. "You're Kiki," he says, then points at Noah. "I can tell by your accessory."

"Good guess," I say with a laugh.

"We only came by to say hello and goodbye to the host," Noah says. "I have plans for this woman."

"Noah!"

Griff laughs. "Oh, really? That's good to hear." He looks at me, his voice lowered as if in confidence. "We have a bet going. Considering how early you two are leaving together, I think I may win the pool."

I can't tell for sure in the dark, but I think Noah blushes, and that possibility amuses me so much that I completely forget to be annoyed.

As for me, I stay quiet, too. I'm afraid of what I might say if I open my mouth. I'd started out so determined to keep my wits and not fall for this man again. And yet I've fallen. Hard.

But I'm still not sure if it's smart to do anything about that.

I'm still pondering that question as we return to the car. Noah opens the door for me and waits until I'm settled before he shuts it. I take a moment alone in the car to sigh. I'd told him years ago that my grandmother's test of a worthy guy was if he opened doors for a woman.

"Where do we have to be?" I ask again when he slides in.

"You'll see."

I turn sideways in my seat and scowl at him. "You do remember me, right? Kiki? We dated in Los Angeles. Almost got married, even."

He pauses before pulling out of into the street. "I have a vague recollection, why?"

"Because I'm the girl who really doesn't like surprises." Surely he remembers that much. Surely he'll tell me where we're going.

But he doesn't. Instead, all he says is, "You'll like this one." Then he pauses. "At least I think you will."

"Noah!"

The smile he flashes is wide and a little smug. "Do you trust me?"

Considering everything in our past, I consider saying no. But I can't. Because somewhere between him leaving me for Darla and now, things have changed. And, yes, I trust him.

Not that I say that. Instead, the words that slip from my lips are, "Dammit, Noah!"

At least he has the grace not to laugh.

Our destination isn't far at all. As the crow flies it's about halfway between his condo and Griffin's house, right downtown on Fourth Street. It's a little bar I've never heard of called Tipsy, and when we step inside, I realize exactly why he's brought me here.

"Oh, no," I say.

"Oh, yes," he counters, tugging my hand.

"Are *you* singing?"

"Trust me. You don't want me to sing."

He snags a recently abandoned table by the stage,

then signals for the waitress. He orders Chardonnay for me, bourbon for him, and then hands the waitress a slip of paper and asks her to put me on the Karaoke performer list.

"You are *so* going to owe me," I say. But my heart isn't in it. I'd had a great time performing at The Fix the other night, and even though a Karaoke bar isn't exactly the Hollywood Bowl, I can't deny that I'm feeling the music—even if I'm cringing at most of the folks who go up to sing.

"This is wretched," I say a half-hour later when a guy who looks like he plays defense for the University of Texas butchers Michael Jackson's *Thriller*.

"I know." Noah grins. "Awesome, isn't it."

I take another sip of my Chardonnay and agree that it is.

"Okay!" The girl in charge of the evening claps as the football player leaves the stage to applause, laughter, and a few catcalls. "And now it's time for Kiki!"

I hurry up front, actually looking forward to it, and hoping I get a song that isn't entirely lame.

The music starts before the lyrics post, and my stomach does a total flip-flop. I stare out at Noah, who's looking smug.

I want to leap off the stage and ask him what he thinks he's doing, but this song is too engrained in me, and I dive into the first verse of *Turnstile* as if I were on autopilot.

This, I know. *This*, I can do.

Soon enough the audience realizes who I am. Then they're standing and clapping and phones are out snapping pictures and, I'm sure, recording every moment.

Celia's probably going to see this on social media before I'm even finished singing.

I don't care. I just want to get lost in the words as I belt out the chorus.

"Turnstile, I slide away,
Turnstile, you'll leave today
Turnstile, I need you now
Turnstile, I don't know how
To love you anymore.
And I go a 'round and around and around and around
And now I know just what I've found.
A man who brings me to my knees.
Baby, baby, please."

I slide back into the chorus, but my eyes never leave Noah's. He's on his feet clapping and laughing and letting out an obscenely loud wolf whistle when I finally finish the song.

"Wow!" The hostess engulfs me in the kind of hug that really doesn't respect personal space, but I'm too pumped to care, and I hug her right back.

"Thank you all," I say into the microphone. "I haven't done that in a long, long time."

A few customers shout for me to do another song, but I shake my head. "Nope, this is Karaoke night. It's someone else's turn."

We stay for at least three more hours, clapping and cheering and rooting all the singers on.

Afterwards, they surround me, telling me how much they loved Pink Chameleon, and asking me to autograph the bar's cardboard coasters.

All in all, it's an incredible night, and I tell Noah as much when we finally step out of the bar and onto the sidewalk.

"I took a chance," he admits. "With all your talk about not rebooting Pink Chameleon, I wanted…"

He trails off, as if not certain what to say.

"What?" I press.

"I wanted you to remember how much you love it."

Tears prick my eyes, and I think that's one of the sweetest things anyone's done for me. "Thank you," I whisper.

"You're welcome."

We walk for a while longer, until I realize that we're not heading toward his car. "Where are we going?"

"Right here," he says, as we reach the corner of Brazos and Sixth. Across the street, the Driskill Hotel stands, proud and lovely.

"Oh." A shiver runs through me, but it's anticipation, not fear. I move closer and slide my arms around his waist. "Noah, I—well, wouldn't you rather go to your place?"

He pulls me close, his strong arms holding me tight against him. "Baby, no. I'm putting you in an Uber."

"What?" I push away, confused.

"I've already called for one. I've had too much to drink to drive you home. I'm just going to leave my car where it is and walk."

"Don't you—I mean—"

I shake my head, confused. I'd been certain he was taking me to a hotel room. I thought he wanted—well, I thought he wanted what I want.

Because I do. Right now, I really want to sleep with this man.

"I can go home with you," I say softly. "I'd like to."

He strokes my hair, his focus on my face. "I'd like nothing more," he says. "But the answer is no."

I start to protest, but he presses a finger against my lips.

"I want you, Kiki. Make no mistake about that. I want you so badly, I ache. But I want all of you, and so I made up my mind. I'm not sleeping with you unless there's more than just sex between us.

"I don't want to be friends with benefits," he continues. "So I'm telling you right now, Kiki, I want more. I want it all. And I'm not a man who settles. Not anymore."

A white Toyota with an Uber placard pulls up, and Noah bends to press a kiss to my forehead. "Your chariot," he says, while I continue to stand mute, overwhelmed by everything he's just said. "I'll see you at work tomorrow."

CHAPTER 17

NOAH GLANCED AT his watch. Two minutes past nine. Which was exactly two minutes later than the last time he'd looked.

And Kiki still wasn't there.

He'd been disappointed to find her office dark when he'd gone early for coffee and pastries, but he'd assumed she slept in. After all, he'd considered doing that very thing, but the allure of seeing her had forced him out of bed and into the kitchen, where four ibuprofens and three cups of coffee had reduced his hangover to a dull throb.

But now his disappointment had turned to worry. He grabbed his phone and called Maia's extension. "Anything?"

"Not in the last fifteen minutes," she said, referring to his previous call. But she didn't sound irritated. On the contrary, she sounded concerned, too. "Hang on," she continued. "We have each other's logon information. I can track her phone."

"Good." He'd intended to do that himself through a few back doors he still had access to from his Deliverance days. He tapped his fingers while he waited for

Maia to report back.

There'd been a few moments when he'd worried that he'd pushed Kiki away last night. That by putting her in the Uber and sending her home, he'd made her rethink their connection and where they might be going personally.

Or, worse, that he'd embarrassed or pissed her off.

None of which were good scenarios, but they were possibilities that he could handle. That *they* could handle. And the moment she arrived in the office, he'd intended to push work aside, sit her down, and have a serious conversation.

That, however, was no longer the nature of his fear. And as he paced in front of his office window, his mind filled with dark images of twisted metal and broken bones and blood spattered on concrete.

Oh, dear God, no…

"Noah?" He'd never heard such a tentative tone in Maia's voice.

"Tell me." He stood stiff, steeling himself against bad news.

"I don't know," she said. "It says her phone's turned off. The last recorded location is South Lamar and Oltorf."

"That's the route she likes to take to downtown," he said. "Down Lamar toward the river."

"Do you think—"

"Mr. Carter?" Carina burst into his office, her face flushed. "Ms. Porter's brother is on line two."

"Maia, I—"

"Yes, go! Call me back."

He pushed the button to switch lines. "What happened? Where is she?"

"She's fine," Cam said. "Banged up, but fine. I'm with her. She's in the ER at Dell," he said, referring to the still-new teaching hospital by the University of Texas campus.

"I tried to call."

"Yeah, well, her phone's in pieces. I'm listed as her emergency contact. Do you want me to—"

"I'll be right there."

"She'll probably be released in a few hours. It's okay. You—"

"I said, I'd be right there."

There was a pause, then Cam said, "Text me when you get here, and I'll tell you how to find us."

Noah scribbled Cam's number, said he'd be there soon, then barked orders at Carina to fill Maia in.

Then he sprinted to the elevator and grabbed a cab at the hotel across the street, because no way was he wasting time going back to his condo for his car.

Downtown abutted the Capital grounds, which bordered on the University, so it didn't take long for him to get to the hospital. He followed Cam's directions and found himself at the nurse's station in the emergency room.

"Kiki Porter," he said, breathless and worried, despite Cam's reassurance that she was fine.

"Noah!"

Cam hurried over before the nurse had finished looking up Kiki's bed number. "She said to tell you that she's okay, and that you're an idiot for leaving the office when there's so much work to be done."

"Screw that," Noah said as they walked the length of curtained ER bays.

"To which I'll reply that I'm sorry if I ripped into you too hard yesterday. As of this moment, you're okay in my book." They paused in front of the curtains surrounding bed number nine. "So don't fuck it up."

"Promise."

Cam nodded, then pulled back the curtain, which clanked as it opened, revealing Kiki's bruised face and embarrassed smile.

Noah grabbed the steel post that formed part of the curtain's railing. He'd been doing fine, but on seeing her, his knees suddenly turned to jelly, and it took all of his effort to stand up and not look like he was gutted.

Because he was.

He hadn't realized it—hadn't let himself feel it—but now that he knew she was safe, it all rushed over him. The realization that he'd come close to losing her a second time. And the certainty that this time, he wouldn't have survived.

"The other guy looks worse," she mumbled, breaking the spell. Her smile was wobbly and her eyes glazed, but she was looking straight at him, as if she understood. "He should. Bastard. It was his fault and he—"

She stopped, her head tilted as she looked at him.

"What?"

She exhaled. "Wow," she breathed. "You look so good." She held out her hand and he took it, then she smiled at Cam. "I told you, right? Why he's special?"

"Kiki." Noah could barely get her name out past the

lump of emotions swelling in his chest. Christ, he needed to get a grip. She needed him to be strong. In control.

"You did," Cam said, shooting Noah a small, amused smile.

She looked at both men. "I'm a little loopy."

His laugh was a relief. "No, really?"

She turned her head, then blinked, obviously trying to focus on Cam. "Now go. Shoo. Time to leave."

"I have a presentation to my advisor in two hours," Cam explained to Noah. "But I've already explained that he'll cut me some slack."

"It's okay," Noah said. "I'll take care of her."

Cam hesitated, shifting from foot to foot.

"Your advisor might cut you some slack, but the rest of the department might not. And I've got this. I'm not leaving until Kiki does, and then she's coming home with me."

"I have a house," she protested, and Noah ignored her.

"I'll text you the elevator code," Noah told Cam. "You can come see her anytime tonight. Seriously. Go."

"Go," Kiki said. "Don't screw up college because I'm all banged up."

"A concussion," Cam corrected. He turned to face Noah. "The doctor said he'd release her so long as someone stayed with her and woke her up throughout the night."

"Done."

He looked over to Kiki, certain she was going to argue ... only to find that she'd drifted off to sleep. He moved to her side, then stroked her hair, his heart twisting. He hated feeling this helpless, this worried.

He might not be able to fix her injuries, but he decided right then and there that he was going to do everything in his power to make sure that she never left his side again.

CHAPTER 18

"HEY. THERE SHE is." Noah's soft voice drifts over me as I force my reluctant eyes to open. "How do you feel?"

I take stock of my body and answer honestly. "Like someone shoved me into an oil barrel and then dropped me from the top of the tower at UT."

"In other words, mild discomfort," he teases, and I hear the relief in his voice. The worry, however, remains in his eyes. He's sitting on the edge of the bed next to me, and he starts to rise as he speaks. "I have your prescription. Let me get you a pill and some water."

"No, that's okay." I'm tired of being drugged up. The entire day is either missing or a blur, and I use my hand to try to push myself up, but I'm too stiff and sore.

"No," he says. "Don't even think about it. Sit back. Relax. Whatever you need done, I can take care of it."

I make a face. "I need to go to the bathroom."

To his credit, he doesn't even crack a smile. "Except that." He shifts, getting his arm around me. "Come on, let's get you up."

He's sweet and gentle, and though I can walk fine— stiff, but fine—he stays with me in case I fall, and then is waiting to walk me back to the bed. I'd inspected myself in the bathroom mirror, and now when I see him, I wince.

"Pain?"

"Just the mental pain of knowing that you're seeing me looking like this." The left side of my face is covered in such a variety of colors I could open my own Sephora. I can't even think about my hair, which is a tangled, unwashed mess. And while my swollen lower lip may be all the rage, I don't think the pouty-lipped look is supposed to feature a scabbed over laceration that bleeds when I smile.

Noah's looking at me like I'm insane, and I lift a shoulder in a shrug, wincing again as I do.

"You're beautiful," he says, with so much sincerity I almost believe him. "Come on."

He leads me back to bed, then tucks me in. "Do you want soup?"

"No, I'm okay."

"Thank God, you are." He gently brushes my hair back, and I lean back against the pillows and sigh, moved by his tenderness and his attention.

"And fair warning, those pills knock you out, and you need more sleep. I'm going to make you take it soon."

"If I get any more sleep, I'll beat out Rip Van Winkle. What time is it, anyway?"

"After midnight."

Surprise rocks me. "Seriously? I slept all day and this late at night?"

He tilts his head, his eyes narrowing. "I take it back.

No more drugs for you."

"Why? What did I say?"

"I've been waking you up about every two hours. You don't remember?"

I think about it, but there's just a big blank. "Nothing."

His green eyes sparkle with mischief. "Such an opportunity and I didn't even know it."

I cross my arms over my chest and try to look affronted. "If you're thinking you could have had your wicked way with me, then you should know that I prefer to be awake for sexy hijinks."

I'm teasing, but as soon as I say the words, I blush. I remember all too well that I came on to him just the other night. And, I remember that he turned me down— in the absolute sweetest of ways.

"I'll keep that in mind," he says, with so much intensity that I blush all over again. "By the way, Ares called. He said to tell you he'll call again tomorrow."

"Did he need to talk to me about his show?" He's got the staging and song order down pat, but for the last two weeks, he's been running tweaks by me.

"Just checking in to see how you're feeling."

"Oh." I wait a second while my fuzzy brain processes that. "Did Cam call him?"

"I did. I got his number from Maia. I thought he'd want to know."

"I can't believe you thought of that. Thank you." I blink, and a tear trails down my cheek. I wipe it away, embarrassed. "Do you have any idea how much I love you right now?"

His eyes widen, and I realize what I've just said.

"I mean, you've been so sweet, taking care of me, and all." I'm trying to cover, even though the truth is that I am falling for him all over again. But I'm not ready to say it out loud, because I'm not ready to risk my heart. "All I've been doing is sleeping—you're the one shouldering everything. Hell, I don't even remember the accident."

He shudders, then reaches for his phone on the bedside table. "A witness sent the responding officer pictures of the scene. He forwarded it to you for insurance." His voice is flat, so tightly controlled it's almost emotionless. "Cam brought your laptop over a few hours ago, and he forwarded the pictures to my phone."

"Bad?" I honestly don't remember, but I can tell from his posture and his voice that it's not just bad, but very bad.

He doesn't answer. Instead, he passes me his phone. There are five pictures, each worse than the one before. The front of my Honda is completely crumpled, and the driver's side door is practically turned inside out.

I feel sick. Because looking at these pictures, I have no idea how I got out of that car alive.

"You slammed into the side window as it shattered, they think. And thank God you had airbags."

"He ran the light," I say, flinching as the memory breaks over me. "I was in the intersection, and..." I trail off, shuddering, then gasp with surprise when he pushes himself violently off the bed and slams his fist into the half wall that separates this area from the rest of the studio.

"Noah!"

"I'm sorry," he says, his back to me, his hands now clenched into fists at his sides.

"I'm sorry," he repeats, and I watch as his posture straightens and he turns to face me. I see the struggle play out over his features, his green eyes haunted.

"What are you sorry for?"

"For this." He indicates himself. "For losing my shit like that. But Kiki…" He trails off, then sits at the foot of the bed and scrubs his hands over his face. He looks tortured, and I hug myself, because I know that I'm the reason.

"I'm fine," I say gently. "It was a horrible wreck, but I'm fine."

"I could have lost you." His voice breaks, and the pain I hear humbles me.

"You didn't." I take his hand and hold it tight. "I'm right here."

His eyes meet mine, and in that moment I regret stumbling backward from my declaration of love. Because it's love that I see in his eyes right now.

"This is twice now that you've proved to be a miracle," he whispers, lifting my hand and gently kissing it.

"What do you mean?" I shift against the pillows, wincing a little.

He frowns. "I'm getting your pill now, whether you like it or not."

I nod in acquiescence, and he heads into the kitchen. Since it's a studio, it's easy enough to hear him.

"I mean that I lost you in Los Angeles, and found you here. Miracle One. And you walked away from that accident with no broken bones or serious injuries. Miracle Two."

"*Lost* me?" I don't mean to sound snippy, but I can't help it.

He returns with my pills and my drink, and I swallow them reluctantly.

"No, you're right," he says. "I didn't lose you. I tossed you away. God, I was so fucking lost back then." He draws a breath. "I've been drowning in guilt for almost ten years now. Guilt that I hurt you, yes. But more than that, guilt that I married Darla. That I stayed with her."

"Because of me?"

"Because she's dead," he snaps, then curses. He draws a breath, and when he speaks again the words come more slowly. Almost eerily slow. "Because if I'd followed my heart—you—then she and Diana would still be alive."

It takes me a moment to follow that chain of reasoning, but when I do, I see where it leads. To Mexico. To anonymous kidnappers. And to a crime that never would have happened had Noah not taken his family on that trip.

"That's not your fault."

"I know that. As far as facts and rational thought go, I'm one hundred percent with you. But in here?" He presses a hand over his heart. "In here, I killed them myself."

"Noah, no…" I don't know what to say. How to make him not feel what he feels. "You can't keep punishing yourself."

"No? I'm doing a remarkable job. Or I was. Then I came here, and I started to heal. I'm not sure if it was the passage of time or closure with Darla's official death declaration or getting out of LA. Whatever it was, this city was working its magic. I was healing."

"I'm glad," I say truthfully. "But why...?"

I trail off.

"Why, what?"

I hesitate, not sure if my question is one to which I truly want an answer. But this may be my only chance to ask him. And even if the answer hurts, I want to know. "Why didn't you come to me after the kidnapping? Was I already so far out of your heart?"

His eyes go wide. "Have you been listening to some other conversation? You *never* left my heart."

"Then, why?"

"How could I do that to you? 'Hi, I love you, I left you, but now I'm back because of a horrible tragedy?'"

"We could have worked through it. Or maybe we couldn't have. But didn't we deserve a chance?"

He drags his hand through his hair. "I don't know. I can look back and see so many possible paths now, but then? Back then I only saw my guilt. And I loved you too damn much to foist that on you. The man you'd fallen in love with was happy. Ambitious. But the guy who returned? Well, he was broken." He meets my eyes. "In a lot of ways he still is."

"Do you think that scares me?"

"I don't know. Maybe it should. But I hope it doesn't, because everything changed for me the day I walked away from a blind date and into The Fix. Because there you were, singing a song about lost love."

I blink as tears prick my eye.

He strokes my right, unbruised cheek, the gentle touch as potent as a kiss. "Like I said, a miracle."

I reach up and press my hand lightly over his, holding his hand against my face. I want so much right now, and yet I don't even know how to put my feelings into words, especially now that the drugs are kicking in and the room is starting to tilt as my eyelids get heavier and heavier.

"Just go to sleep," he says, stroking my hair and guiding me down so that my head is on the pillow. "I'll be right here."

"I know you will."

He presses a kiss to my forehead, and I force my eyes to flutter open.

"Noah? Can I go with you? To LA?"

"You want to meet Ryan? About the security system testimonials?"

That's not what I mean, and for a second, his words make no sense. Then I remember Red Brick and the job and all the rest of it. "I just meant for the wrap party," I say sleepily. "I'd like to go. As your date, I mean. If that's okay."

I force my eyes back open so I can see him, and I'm rewarded by a joyous smile.

"Baby, that sounds perfect to me."

CHAPTER 19

"I CAN'T BELIEVE we're on a studio backlot. Look!" I say, pointing at the fake facade of a two-story house. "I know I've seen that house in some television show. No," I correct. "A movie. Definitely a movie."

I'm not a celebrity hound, but I can't deny that being on the backlot with the likes of Hollywood A-listers like Lyle Tarpin and Francesca Muratti is pretty damn amazing. And even though I'm trying not to be a drooling fan girl, I think I'm losing the battle.

"You're cute when you're awed," Noah says. To which I stick out my tongue. In the most polite way, of course.

"But seriously," I say, hooking my arm through his as I gaze over the crowd and the set pieces for *M. Sterious,* the blockbuster action movie that will be released next year. "This is pretty much the best date ever."

"Better than miniature golf?"

I lift myself up on my tiptoes and press a quick kiss to his cheek. "Nothing's better than miniature golf."

He laughs, then raises his hand to wave at someone across the crowd.

And there really is a crowd.

In addition to everyone who worked on the film, the cast and crew invited their own friends and family. And on top of that, Lyle invited fifty kids enrolled in various programs offered by the Stark Children's Foundation, an organization that assists abused, traumatized and disenfranchised children through sports and play therapy, though lately its mission has expanded to include mentoring.

All of which I know because Lyle and Damien explained it when we first arrived, after being shuttled from the airport to the studio in a private car from Stark's fleet. Another perk that I could get used to.

Lyle is active in the organization and acts as a Youth Advocate, which is more than just a mentor. Instead, Youth Advocates are celebrities who publicly share their own past trauma in order to help the kids in the program realize that they're not alone.

"You should consider doing it," Lyle tells Noah, when he and his girlfriend, Sugar, come over to greet us. "There's power in owning the shit from your past. And a lot of these kids have lost family members through violence. You've got a lot to offer them."

"We'll see," Noah says, as Sugar hip bumps Lyle even as she shoots me an amused glance. Her eyes are brown, a shade similar to mine, but no freckles dot her nose, and her hair is the kind of blonde that reminds me of beaches and summer.

I remember that there was some sort of media brouhaha that involved the two of them a few months ago, but I don't recall any of the details, other than that I thought it was unfair that she'd had her privacy ripped away. It wasn't as if she'd jumped into the spotlight on purpose, like Celia and I were hoping to do with Pink Chameleon.

But I suppose that's the price Sugar paid dating a guy whose face often peers out at the world from magazines in supermarket checkout lines. From the expression on her face when she looks at him, I'm certain she thinks it was worth the price.

"This is supposed to be a party, not a recruitment event," Sugar continues. "So behave."

"Only if I get to misbehave later," Lyle says with a wink.

"I think that can be arranged."

Lyle catches Noah's eye and grins. Then he turns his attention to me. "Come on. I'll introduce you to Francesca."

"Muratti?" If Lyle's a star, Francesca Muratti is a supernova. "Really?"

"I told her you were coming. She's a fan." He glances around. "Where did Celia go?"

Noah had asked Lyle to invite her, and she'd completely squealed over him when we'd first arrived, then almost lost her shit when he'd autographed her T-shirt. Now, I look around and find her talking to a stunning brunette with a microphone. She sees me and waves, her shoulder-length pink curls bouncing.

"Who's she talking to?" I ask Lyle, but it's Noah who answers. "That's Jamie Archer. Well, Jamie Hunter, now."

"You know her?" Considering he just told me she

was married, the tinge of jealousy is ridiculous.

"She's Nikki Stark's best friend. And she recently married Ryan Hunter."

"The Stark security chief that you want to talk to about beta-testing?"

"Right," Noah said. "He's around here somewhere. We'll find him later," he adds as Celia rushes up and grabs my arm.

"That's Jamie Archer," she says. "She does entertainment reporting, and I told her we're getting Pink Chameleon back together. I think she might do a story on us!"

"That's fabulous!" I don't tell her that since Jamie is friends with the Starks, that it's a solid bet Noah can pull some strings to make that happen for sure. Celia's too proud of herself for having snagged such a potential PR coup.

"Right now, Lyle wants us to meet Francesca Muratti."

As I expect, her jaw drops. "No way."

"She's a fan," Lyle says, then waves. "And here she comes." He indicates the famous brunette who's now walking next to a god of a man with chestnut hair, broad shoulders, a wide mouth, and hard, assessing eyes. He looks like a man used to giving orders. More important, he looks like a man who expects them to be followed.

"Holy fu-*dge*" Celia says, correcting herself as one of the SCF kids scurries past us.

"It was sweet of you to let the kids be extras," I say to Lyle, as Celia gapes at Francesca and her companion. Noah and I had come straight from the airport, and while the cast and crew shot the last scene with the kids as extras, Lyle had one of the makeup artists do my face, a favor for which I will be forever grateful. I'd been excited about the party, but not about my lingering bruises. And she'd managed to cover every one of them.

"That's Holt," Celia whispers. "Holy crap we're going to meet Francesca Muratti and Matthew Holt at the same time. I think I'm going to throw up."

"You are not," I order, then smile as they approach, even though my stomach's turning flip-flops, too. "Hi, I'm Kiki, and this is Celia. Lyle says you're a fan of our music," I say to Francesca, "which is so amazing because we're both huge fans of yours. I mean, your films are so—*ow*."

I stop rambling when Celia kicks me, after which I can't decide if I'd rather die of embarrassment or kick her back.

"It's great to meet both of you," she says, taking it all in stride. Noah's beside me now, and she turns her attention to him. "And great to see you again. Lyle says you're in Austin now. That's one of my favorite towns."

"You'll have to come visit sometime," Noah says. "Maybe South By Southwest," he adds, mentioning the popular festival for music and more.

"That could be fun," she says. "You two are really putting Pink Chameleon back together? Lyle said so, but he knows I'm a fan, and I wouldn't put it past him to tease me. Any chance you'll be performing at South By?"

Celia and I exchange looks, and I'm sure I look just as awed as she does. "Oh," I finally say. "Um."

Which was not my finest conversational moment,

but it's better than Celia's wide-eyed silence.

"These two are part of the group you wanted to tell me about?" Holt asks Francesca. It's a simple question, but there's an edge to it that makes me believe the stories about Holt. The man's got drive and talent and a boatload of money—but he's damaged goods.

"Oh, yes. I think you'll be impressed."

"I already am," Holt says. "Which one of you is Celia?"

Beside me, Celia squeaks, but manages to cover by pretending to cough. "That's me."

"You're the one who sent me the track?"

"I-um, yeah."

He glances at Francesca. "You're right. I'm impressed." He shifts his focus and nods at both Celia and me. "I don't know how you got my personal email address, but send more. And I'll be in touch."

He turns and walks away, and for a moment it's all I can do to breathe. Then Celia does a fist pump before scooping me into a hug. I hug her back, and we dance around like idiots, but the second she releases me, I launch myself into Noah's arms. He twirls me around, then kisses me—hard and fast and intoxicating. But not enough. Not nearly enough.

"Noah," I say, my voice cracking on his name. I love Celia. I love that we have this chance.

But right now, it's Noah I want to celebrate with.

He's looking at me like he wants to devour me, and I think that's the best idea ever. "We're still working together," he murmurs, his voice pitched only for me.

I draw in a breath, because that's a line I didn't want

to cross. But with Noah, the lines are already blurred. We never spoke of it, but it happened. We're together. We're *us*.

And right now, all I want is him.

"I don't care," I whisper.

I see the heat in his eyes. The need. And I know that there is no way in hell we're staying through the end of this party.

Celia knows it, too, and she steps forward with one hand on her hip, tilts her head back, and looks Noah in the eye. "I've always liked you," she says. "Back then, before all the shit went down, I thought you were good for her. And even though I wanted to fucking kill you when you hurt my girl, I kinda got why you did it. Doesn't make you not an asshole, but I kinda understood.

"But I'm telling you right now that if you hurt her again, I'm going to rip your nuts off." She smiles prettily. "I just want to be clear."

"My nuts and I thank you for the warning." His gaze shifts to me. "I promise, it won't be necessary."

"Hmm."

"Later," I say, resisting the urge to roll my eyes at my friend.

"Tomorrow," she says. "Lunch. Your hotel. Both of you. We have catching up and planning to do. 'Cause we're gonna be so famous. Matthew Fucking Holt," she says. "I can't even."

Since I can't either, we grab each other and hug again. And when she releases me, she whispers, "I wasn't sure about him being back, but I think it's good."

"I know it is," I say, then give her another squeeze before I pull away. Noah takes my hand, and we start toward the exit.

We don't, however, make it. We're stopped by Lyle's voice over the loudspeaker, and when we look for the source, we see that he's standing on a makeshift stage near the craft services table. Most of the guests surround him, including the SCF kids.

"I have a couple of very special announcements," he says, and Noah catches my eye, his look a question.

I want to leave, but I don't want to be rude. And so I shrug, disappointed, and hold onto his hand as we listen to Lyle give a quick speech about SCF, the kids, and the Youth Advocate program.

"He's right," I say "You'd be a benefit to the program."

"It's on my radar," Noah says, and I know better than to push. Instead, we listen to the rest of Lyle's speech. When he's done, he thanks everyone for coming, then asks for a few more minutes of our attention.

"We have something special to announce," Lyle says, holding his hand out to Sugar, who joins him on the stage. "Last night, I asked the love of my life, Sugar Laine, to marry me. And I'm thrilled to announce that she said yes."

The audience erupts, and when Lyle pulls Sugar close and kisses her very thoroughly, a few catcalls and wolf whistles are added to the mix.

When the crowd dies down and Lyle and Sugar come off the stage to mingle, we go over to congratulate them and say goodbye. "You inspired us to go celebrate,"

Noah says, looking at me with such obvious heat and purpose I can feel my blush rise.

"It was great meeting you," I tell Sugar as I hug her and Lyle goodbye in turn. "And congrats again."

Once again, we head for the exit gate, and once again, we're stopped. This time by Damien, who's accompanied by his wife, Nikki, a former Texas beauty queen, who I recognize from years of seeing the two of them in magazines and on the internet.

"Heading out?" Damien asks after introductions are made all around.

"We have some plans this evening," Noah says, and I try to keep my expression bland, so as to not telegraph exactly what kind of plans he's talking about.

"I won't take up much of your time, but in case you're planning on working tonight—" His expression suggests that he knows very well that we won't be. "—I wanted to tell you to hold off. I've been talking with the CEO of the Israeli company, and for a variety of reasons, we're considering a co-venture."

"Oh." Noah catches my eye and frowns. "What does that mean for us?"

"It means we're putting the marketing on hold." He turns to me. "We'll pay out the full contract with Crown Consulting, of course. And we'll bring Crown back on board when the new deal is ironed out, if your schedule permits."

"Wow," I say. "Thank you." Not only for the promise of future work, but because a lot of companies would have haggled over whether full payment for this contract was still due, and under the situation he describes, it's a close question. I appreciate Stark not fighting that battle, especially since the income is so important to me.

"Is this because of the possible leaks?" Noah asks. "Because I've been meaning to mention something."

Damien frowns. "Not directly. But what's going on?"

Noah tells him about the green pickup truck that he keeps seeing near his condo and office. "It's probably nothing to do with Red Brick. But it's bothering me, so I thought I'd mention it."

"Doubtful it's relevant," Damien says. "But I'll have someone check it out."

Noah nods, and Nikki steps closer to me. "I wanted to say I'm sorry we didn't get a chance to talk more, but I'm sure we'll see each other again."

"Enjoy your evening," Damien says as he puts his arm around Nikki and pulls her close. The intimacy between them is so palpable it makes my heart ache, and without thinking, I reach out and take Noah's hand. *That's what I want*, I think. *That's how I feel.*

I tilt my head to see him looking at me, his face a mirror of my emotions.

And that's the moment it happens.

That's the moment that I know we'll be okay.

IT TAKES EVERY ounce of self-control I have not to jump Noah in the elevator. I want him. I want to feel his body pressed against mine. I want to feel his mouth on me. I want his cock inside me.

I want to close my eyes and give myself over to his

pleasure.

In short, I want to be *his*.

I'm a bubbling mess of need by the time we finally stumble out of the elevator car and down the hall toward his room. He fumbles in his pocket, then presses the key against the magnetic pad.

Nothing happens.

We look at each other, and when he mutters, "Come on, you fucker," as he tries again, I know for certain that he's as desperate as I am to get inside.

This time, thankfully, the key works, and he shoves the door open, then takes my hand and pulls me into the room with him.

"I was starting to—" I begin, but I don't finish the thought, because Noah has me pressed up against the wall, his mouth silencing me in a kiss, his hands moving over my hair, my face, my breasts.

"Finally," he says, when he comes up for air. "Do you know how long I've waited to touch you like this?"

I laugh, delighted by the fact that he's just as crazed as I am. "I'd say exactly as long as I've waited. And please, please Noah, don't make me wait any longer."

"Hell, no," he says.

I'm wearing a thin cotton button down paired with a knit skirt. And even as he speaks, his hands find the collar. He pulls hard in opposite direction, sending buttons flying as the shirt tears open, revealing my pale, pink bra.

I gasp, then laugh.

"Don't say a word," he orders. "I don't care if you liked it. I'll buy you a dozen more. I have to have you. I have to taste you."

"I did like it," I say. "But I like what you just did better."

His eyes meet mine, and the slow curve of his smile sends liquid heat coursing through me. I press my legs together. I'm so wet I can feel it on my thighs, and I know the miniscule bit of material that forms the crotch of my thong panties is already thoroughly soaked.

As if he can read my thoughts, he tugs the skirt down. The elastic waistband stretches easily, and it slides over my hips, revealing my panties—or, more accurately, revealing me. Because the panties aren't much more than damp material. He tugs them down and tosses them to the side, then orders me to take off my bra.

I do, but when I start to drop it on the ground, he takes it from me, then starts to wrap it around my wrists.

"What are you doing?"

"What I wanted to do in my condo, but what we weren't ready for."

"Oh." I lick my lips, thinking back to that night and talk of trust and commitment. My heart swells with hope. "We're ready now?"

His green eyes meet mine, and I think I can see all the way to his soul. "Oh, yes."

He leads me to the bed, then looks at me with a frown. "Damn hotels. There's no place to secure it."

He's right. The headboard is padded and apparently screwed to the wall.

With a rakish grin, he trails a fingertip down my naked body, from my collar bone to my clit.

I gasp, my breath shuddering, my legs wobbling.

"Can I trust you to be good?"

I nod. But honestly, right then, I'd say just about anything.

Then I frown, because I realize I'm not sure what *good* means. Not in this context.

He chuckles, obviously understanding my confusion. "I wanted to tie you down, but I can't. So I need you to stretch out. Hands above your head. I want you to mimic being bound."

He nods toward the bed, and I climb on, then do as he says.

"Beautiful." He bends over and brushes a light kiss over my lips. "It's important because I want to look at you and know that you're mine. I want you vulnerable, open to me. I want the trust, Kiki."

His fingertips dance over my skin as he speaks, as if his words are only the melody and he's using the connection between my body and his for the harmony.

"I want to look at you and know that I'm the only man with the privilege of seeing you naked and vulnerable. The only man who can touch you. And I want you to give yourself to me, knowing that I will never want another woman. I want your surrender, baby. Basically, I want all of you."

He is still clothed, and the brush of his jeans against my bare hips as he straddles me is wildly erotic. "Tell me, baby," he says, as he bends forward, running his hands up my body and cupping my breasts. "Do you want that, too?"

"Yes. Oh, God, yes."

"Do you want me now?"

"You know I do."

"Are you wet for me?"

I spread my legs, the cool air magnificent against my heated core. "Find out."

He chuckles. "I think I will. And here's the other thing, baby," he says, as presses his lips to my stomach. He tilts his head up just enough to look at me. "The most important thing. I want to take us both as high as we can go, and if we crash back down to earth, I want to know that we're here to catch each other."

"Noah…" His name is like breath on my lips. His words have started me melting, and now his kisses down to my core are about to finish me off.

He brings his hands down, then eases two fingers inside me as his tongue strokes my clit.

I buck, gasping with pleasure. "Noah—oh, yes."

"Do you like that?"

"Can't you tell?" I bring my hands down, wanting my fingers in his hair.

"No," he said. "No touching. This is all on me. There's something I want to give you."

He knows exactly how to tease me. Where to suck. Where to thrust. Where to lave me until I'm on the edge and then pull back to leave me trembling and needy.

He plays me like a fine instrument, and only when my body is perfectly tuned and ready does he finally push me over the edge so that I break apart, crying his name as the world turns inside out and colored sparks fill my vision.

He slides up beside me, holding me as the last tremors spread through my body. Then he releases my wrists and I roll over to face him with a satisfied smile.

"Was that what you wanted to give me? An incredible orgasm?"

"Not exactly."

I don't understand what he means, and I'm even more confused when he gets off the bed and goes to the hotel dresser, then comes back with something hidden in his fist.

"I'm not giving this to you now," he says. "I don't want to rush. But I want to give you the promise of it now."

I frown, still confused. "The promise of what?"

"The world," he says, and opens his hand. "*Our* world."

There, on his palm, is the ring he gave me a decade ago in Los Angeles. The engagement ring I threw at him in anger when he left me for Darla.

My hand flies to my mouth, and when I look at him, it's through eyes filled with tears. "I don't understand. You're *not* giving this to me?"

"Not yet. This isn't a proposal." His mouth curves up. "But I wanted you to know that a proposal—and the ring—is coming. Until then, I hope you keep it in your heart. And here," he adds, then takes my left hand and kisses the place where the ring will be.

I swallow through a throat clogged with tears. "I think that's the most romantic thing anyone has ever done." I lean forward, then kiss him tenderly. "Will you do something for me?"

"Anything."

"Make love to me, Noah. Slowly. And very, very thoroughly."

"Sweetheart, it will be my pleasure."

CHAPTER 20

H E DIDN'T REMEMBER falling asleep, but waking up was a pleasure. The brush of Kiki's hair over his skin. The soft pressure of her lips against his bare chest. Her naked body straddling him as she sweetly kissed her way higher and higher until she finally claimed him with the kind of kiss designed to make a man come awake.

Very awake.

With a low growl, he pulled her to him, then shifted his weight to flip them over. She squealed and laughed, now flat on her back and pinned beneath him.

"Don't start what you can't finish," he teased.

"Oh, no, mister. That was a wake-up call, not a booty call. Because we're due downstairs in twenty minutes, and I'm not going without my faux-ancé."

"Your what?"

"Fake fiancé," she explained. "Except not truly fake. So maybe *pre*-ancé?"

He wasn't sure if he should laugh or kiss her, so he settled for both, and only stopped because she wrestled her way out from under him, then grabbed him by the hand. "I promise to make it up to you later," she said. "But right now, we're supposed to have lunch with Celia.

It's important."

"I know. I'll be good." He grinned as he slid off the bed, pulling her to her feet beside him. "And when we get back to the room, I'll be better."

"I like that plan." She wrapped her arms around him, her warm, naked body pressed against his. "Thank you."

He slid his hands down, cupping her bare ass and pulling her tight against him, so that there was no way she could miss how hard he was. "Thank me later," he whispered, the took her mouth in a slow, soft kiss.

When they broke apart, she was a little glassy eyed, which was fine with him. She hurried to get dressed, and though he considered joining her in the shower, they both knew that would only make them late. That would be fine with him, too—hell, it would be fine with him to cancel. Not because he didn't like Celia, but because he hadn't yet had his fill of Kiki.

Then again, he doubted he'd ever have his fill of her.

But late would irritate Celia, and at the moment, Noah was all about ensuring that he continued to have the approval of Kiki's best friend.

They found her at a table with a view of the city. The hotel's restaurant was on the top floor, and boasted both ocean and inland views. "Wasn't yesterday the most freaking amazing day ever?" Celia asked as she hugged each of them in turn. "Matthew Holt likes us. He really likes us!"

"I know!" Kiki's voice held the same level of excitement as Celia's, and Noah basked in their joy as they spun out plans and dreams. They'd make it—he firmly believed that.

Hell, they would have made it before if he hadn't broken Kiki's spirit and shattered her drive.

But that wasn't a problem this time.

This time, he wasn't going anywhere.

When the girls wound down, Kiki leaned against him as they scoped out the menu, then ordered. The waitress left, and Celia started to outline the day. "Eden and Kristi can't make it here this weekend, but you and I can clean up a few of the melodies for the lyrics you sent over last, and then we can record some tracks together. I went ahead and booked some studio time."

Celia looked at Noah, as if daring him to raise alternative plans.

"Sounds great to me. You two mind if I watch?"

Celia caught Kiki's eye, and then looked back to Noah. "Do you really want to, or are you just trying to make sure things are right between us?"

"Both."

She pressed her lips together, then nodded slowly. "Gotta give the guy points for honesty. Okay, then. But when we ask for your opinion it has to be real. Empty platitudes don't help us sell records."

"I'll be a totally critical bastard," he promised, managing not to crack a smile.

"All right, then. That's the plan."

They didn't talk much once the food came. They were all eager to get out of there and get to the studio. Noah left cash, then slid out of the booth, extending his hand to help Kiki.

Which was why he was facing the wrong direction when Celia said, "Um, I think they're coming for you."

He frowned, then turned to see Damien Stark, Ryan Hunter, and Dallas Sykes walking toward him. Which made no sense. As far as Noah knew, Dallas was in London. If he'd returned early, he surely would have been at the wrap party last night, especially since Jane, his wife, had written the book and screenplay that was the basis of Lyle's first break-out role.

"Hey man," Dallas said, his usually *GQ*-ready face looking haggard. An heir to billions, Dallas was also the founder of Deliverance. He'd seen more than his share of tragedy and been run through the public gossip mill more times than Noah could count. So the fact that he looked so drawn and exhausted concerned Noah more than his unexpected and unexplained presence in the restaurant.

"How did you know we were here?"

"It's important," Dallas said. "I had Quincy trace your cell phone."

Noah was still holding Kiki's hand. Now, he tightened his grip, as if to ensure she was safe. Quincy was MI-6, and also part of the Deliverance team. If Dallas was pulling him in for an unauthorized trace, it was even more serious than he thought.

"You could have texted," he said, warily. "I wasn't hiding."

Then he realized he'd left his phone in the room. Which meant that whatever was going on, his friends didn't want to wait until he saw and returned the text.

"Who are you? And what's going on?" Kiki asked, voicing the question that Noah was avoiding. Because something deep in his gut told him that he didn't want to hear the answer. Because the answer would destroy everything.

"This is Dallas Sykes," Damien said, introducing him, and Noah knew from the way Kiki squeezed his hand that she recognized the name.

"Let's move to the patio," Noah said, feeling both on display and claustrophobic.

The main portion of the restaurant took up most of the top floor. But it also featured a small patio on the west side with no seating, and they all went there now, the view of the ocean a stunning counterpart to the ominous conversation.

"I asked Ryan to look into your green pickup last night," Damien continued, smoothly picking up the conversation. "And based on what he learned, I asked Dallas to come."

"You were in London."

"Yeah," Dallas said. "Well…"

"Tell me." Noah's throat felt thick. Behind him, he heard Celia move to Kiki's other side and take her hand.

Damien glanced at Kiki, then at Noah. "Do you want—"

"She stays," he says. "They both do," he added, not wanting to deny Kiki the support of her best friend, whatever this was about.

Damien nodded, then gestured to Ryan.

"I called a friend of mine in Austin, Pierce Blackwell," Ryan said. "He has a security company, and I asked him and his partners to see what they could learn about the pickup. I thought they'd have to pull traffic and security cam footage and do some serious looking, but it turns out it was parked right outside your building."

A wave of dread slammed against Noah. "This doesn't have anything to do with Red Brick, does it?"

"It doesn't." Dallas shoved his hands in his pockets, looking nervous. Another bad sign.

"Just tell me," Noah demanded.

"It's Darla," Dallas said flatly, as the ground fell out from under Noah. "Darla's the woman in the pickup."

CHAPTER 21

*D*ARLA.

The name settles on me like a ghost, and I back away without thinking—then realize with despair how easily Noah lets my fingers slip out of his grip.

Darla.

It's like a nightmare. No, it *is* a nightmare.

Behind me, Celia puts her hand on my shoulder, and though I welcome her steadying presence, it's not her touch I crave. But Noah hasn't reached for me. He hasn't done anything. He's just standing there, as if Dallas is speaking in an ancient language that Noah can't comprehend.

Finally, I manage to speak. "You're sure? It's really her? Not some con artist trying to fuck with him?"

"It's her," Dallas says.

My chest aches and my skin turns clammy. Icy fear settles over me, and it's all I can do not to let everyone see the way I'm shaking. But dammit, I'm going to be strong.

Noah turns then and looks at me, his expression more lost than I've ever seen. I hate myself right now, and I move back to his side and press my right hand to the small of his back. He needs as much strength as I can give him. This is a shock, but it doesn't change anything. He's moved on with his life.

The problem is that I'm afraid that he's going to slide backwards.

Yes, it's a miracle that she's alive, but I can't deny that I'm scared. Because she's a threat. She's the enemy, just like she was all those years ago when she took him away from me.

Except she's not, and I need to push past that fear. This is *now*, not ten years ago.

Noah and I have both grown so much since Los Angeles, and even though this is a shock, I'll be by his side, and we'll get through it together.

I rub my left ring finger, remembering the love in his eyes when he told me that one day he'd give me the ring for real.

I tell myself this doesn't change anything.

But the truth is, I don't believe myself.

My thoughts are churning. And right now, I'm so very scared.

"You checked DNA," Noah finally says, and his low, raw voice reminds me of a wounded animal. "It's been barely any time, but Deliverance has the resources to act fast. You did, didn't you? There's no doubt. Otherwise, you wouldn't be here." He looks at Dallas. "Would you?"

The tiny movement of Dallas's head is barely a nod. "There's no doubt."

Noah opens his mouth, as if to ask a question, then closes it again.

I step forward. "Why now? What happened? How did she survive? Why is she back?" The questions roll off my tongue, followed by the one I've been trying the hardest not to think about. "Are they still married?"

"I've asked Charles—my attorney—to look into that," Damien says. And the fact that the answer isn't a simple *no* weighs heavy on me.

"As for the other questions," Dallas says, "I asked her that on the phone." His focus is on Noah. "She says she'll tell you everything. But only you, at least at first."

He nods. "Okay, then. I'll go back to Austin tonight. Damien, I know it's not company business, but can I use one of the Stark jets?"

"Of course," Damien says.

"But you're not going to Austin," Ryan puts in. "We offered to fly her out here to meet you, but she turned us down. She said she's driving back to Oklahoma City. She should be there by now."

"That's where she was from," Noah says, as if that is more convincing evidence than DNA.

"We checked that out, too," Dallas says. "Her mother's still there in a small house outside of town. No income other than her disability check. Darla's father passed away five years ago with no assets and no insurance. As far as we could tell, Darla showed up on her doorstep a few months ago, then drove down to Austin more recently to look for you."

"Why go back?" I ask. "If she was desperate to see Noah, why leave now that she's found him?"

Dallas frowns, but doesn't answer. And before I can press the question, Noah looks at him, his expression tortured. "All that time with Deliverance searching for victims, and I never found her."

"Noah, don't." Dallas's voice is firm. "You joined Deliverance long after Darla disappeared. She was never one of our cases. And even if you would sometimes look, follow a lead, whatever, the fact is you didn't have all the information."

"I knew where she went missing. I knew where Diana's body was found." His voice is as hard as stone. As if every syllable is painful.

"You were looking for a woman alone," Dallas says with the unnaturally stiff posture of someone delivering a devastating blow. "And you were expecting to find a path to a body, not to a survivor."

"Alone," Noah repeats, his voice wary. "What do you mean?"

"She says she has a son. She says he's yours."

Noah stumbles, and I hold my hand out to steady him, feeling horribly unstable myself. Like I've been thrown back ten years, and it's happening all over again.

"Mine? That's impossible."

Dallas draws a breath. "He's almost nine, Noah. If Darla was newly pregnant when she was kidnapped, then it's possible. The boy could be yours."

I'M NUMB AS we go back to the hotel room to pack. We both are. We move like zombies through the room, gathering our things.

The air is cloying, as if it holds even more horrible

surprises, and although I try to talk to Noah, he's lost in silence. When he does speak, it's only in monosyllables.

"Noah, please." I'm sitting on the edge of the bed, my small carry-on bag already packed. "You should talk about it. You'll feel better."

"Will I?" he snaps. "Talking will make me feel better about leaving my pregnant wife behind in Mexico? About not looking for her hard enough when I had all the resources at my disposal to do that?"

I cringe, not only from the force of his words, but from the pain within them. But it's the most words he's spoken since we arrived in the room, and I try to hold onto that fact as a mini-victory.

"It's not your fault," I say. But the look he gives me makes perfectly clear that he doesn't agree with that at all.

"What are you going to do?" I ask.

"Make it better." His voice is laced with a fierce determination, and I'm struck by a sudden, horrible memory. *I have to make it right,* he'd said to me ten years ago. *I have to make it better.*

"Noah," I begin, but I can't go on. My throat is too full of tears and the past is pushing painfully against me. I force myself to breathe, then try again, hoping desperately that I'm not looking down the path that we're about to travel. One we walked already, ten years ago.

Finally, I manage to form one simple question. "How?"

"I don't know," he says. "Whatever it takes to make it right."

I swallow, then nod numbly, my worst fears confirmed. I've lived this nightmare before, and I know where it's going. I blink back tears, hoping that I'm wrong. Hoping that everything we've rebuilt hasn't just crumbled into dust around us.

"We should go," I say.

He picks up his bag and swings the strap over his arm. For the first time, his eyes seem clear as he looks at me. "Kiki, oh, God, Kiki. I'm so sorry."

He moves closer, then brushes away the tears that are trailing down my cheek. "But I need to go do this alone."

CHAPTER 22

"I'M FINE," I lie, as I pull Celia's snuggly purple blanket up around my shoulders. "You didn't have to put me up tonight. The hotel would have been fine."

"Fine?" she repeats. "Do you know what a completely lame word that is? Because seriously, sweetie, unless you define *fine* by whether or not you're on this earth and breathing you are not fine at all."

I grimace. "Well, that's something at least."

She makes a scoffing sound. "You can stay here as long as you want, you know. Hang out. We'll write songs. Drink buckets of wine. Eat cookies. My couch is yours for as long as you need it."

Her apartment in Culver City is small, about the size of Noah's place. Only hers isn't a studio, but a one-bedroom. Which means her room is tiny and the living room is tiny.

Right now, I'm in the tiny living room on a tiny couch while Celia sits in front of me on her tiny coffee table.

It feels a lot like we're camping out inside a doll-house.

"I appreciate the offer," I say. "But honestly, I just

want to get home."

She nods slowly. "Because you have such an intense work schedule planned out? I thought as of yesterday you were contract-less."

"Do I have to be going home for work? Maybe I want to see my place. Or maybe I want to get with Maia and put together some new proposals. Strike while the iron is hot. Or maybe I want to drive up to Dallas and do a couple of shows with Seven Percent before we get churning on Pink Chameleon."

"Really?" Her brows lift. "Do you?" She stands, then moves into her surprisingly roomy kitchen, keeping an eye on me as she walks.

I lift a shoulder, feeling trapped. "Maybe."

She pulls a corkscrew out of a drawer and waves it at me before violently attacking a bottle of Chardonnay. "You're a piece of work," she says. "You know that, right?"

I pull my knees up and tug the blanket tighter around me. "I don't know what you're talking about."

"The hell you don't. Come on, Keeks, I know how you are. You don't look at the future through rose-colored glasses. To you, it's all baby shit brown."

"Ew. And again, *ew*."

She's unrepentant as she brings me a glass of wine. "Maybe, but accurate."

"No, it's not. I'm pragmatic, that's all."

"Really? Because going to Dallas and joining Seven Percent makes so much sense when Noah's going to be back."

I look down into my wine. I don't want to do this; I

just want to sleep and wake up and have the world be back the way I want it.

"Dammit, Keeks. Things are not crap right now." She leaves her wine on the coffee table and sits down on the couch beside me, then takes my hand. "I mean, come on. For one thing, Pink Chameleon is about to rock the music world, right? We have Matthew Holt interested, our sound is amazing. And you know that. You know it's going to happen, you just don't want to admit it."

"It should happen," I agree. "But not everything turns out the way it should. Most things don't." I think of Noah right beside me just yesterday, talking about rings and futures. And then everything shifted, and suddenly it was ten years ago all over again.

"Noah loves you," she says, reading my mind as only a best friend can. "You're just scared."

"I'm terrified," I admit. What I don't say out loud is that I'm also angry. He was mine again—for a few, wonderful days, he was really and truly mine. And then *she* came in and stole him away a second time. And I can't even hate her. Not after what's happened to her. Not after everything she's lost.

Celia squeezes my hand. "Do you really want to be someone who lives their life anticipating the worst?"

"No." The word comes out hoarse because of the unexpected tears that suddenly clog my throat. "No," I repeat, my voice stronger. "But this is what happens. The world doesn't care what I think, and the people in it make decisions without me. My world changes, and I don't get a say in it."

"But you do," she says firmly.

I just tilt my head and start to count on my fingers. "Really? My dad. My stepfather. My mom. They just left. They just walked. And then Noah and Darla. He didn't even ask what I thought. Didn't ask if I understood. And after she was kidnapped, he didn't come find me. He said he didn't want to burden me with his guilt. His suffering. He made the goddamn decision for me."

"Because you didn't fight." She pushes up off the couch and starts to pace. "You didn't fight, and I don't get it. Because you're the strongest fighter I know. You built Crown Consulting out of nothing. You practically forced your way back to your music even when you didn't have to. You didn't have any illusions about reforming PC when you started writing again. You were just fighting to get back something you love."

She's right. I know she is, even though it's hard to think about how I've sat back and allowed things to happen to me without trying to battle them back.

And no, I couldn't have fought for my dad or my step-dad or my mom. I was too young. They left, I had no way of fighting, and that impotence scarred me.

But I could have fought for Noah. When Darla told him she was pregnant, I should have jumped into the ring. Instead, I lingered on the sideline until Noah told me that he was marrying her. Even then, I didn't fight. Not really. I numbly accepted his decision, even though it was so damn wrong for both of us.

And Owen—I'd done the opposite of fight. He'd started talking about moving out of state, and I began to suspect that he was seeing Abby behind my back. And rather than fight, I just pulled the plug.

With him, though, it didn't haunt me, because the sad truth is, I didn't love him enough to fight for.

Not the way I love Noah.

"This is torture," I whisper. "And you're right." I stand up as she sits down, and now it's my turn to pace. "I *am* a fighter. I pulled out all the stops to get that Stark contract, and then Darla came waltzing back into town, and suddenly I'm back in Los Angeles all those years ago. And she's running to him again, and she has a kid again.

"And I'm sitting on my ass again," I continue, "not doing a thing. And damn sure not fighting."

"Do you honestly think it's the same this time?" she asks. "Do you truly believe he'll leave you?"

"Yes. No." I drag my fingers through my disheveled hair in a very Noah-like manner. "I don't know. My heart can't believe it, but my head can't help but fear it. And either way, I'm pissed off. Because he's making the rules, and I'm sure he thinks he's protecting me, but that's not what he gets to do. If we're a couple, then we need to be a couple."

"And there you go," Celia says smugly. "That's the fight."

"Yes," I say, looking blankly around the room, not even sure what I'm searching for. And then I realize. "Where's my purse? I can't get to Oklahoma without my purse."

"Oh," she says innocently. "Are you going somewhere?"

"I'm going to be there to support him, to help him, whether he wants me to or not. His goddamn guilt be damned."

"Good for you."

"And if we're not still a couple—"

"Don't even go there," she says, sticking her fingers in her ears.

I smirk and stay quiet. But in my head, I make a pledge. He's not getting rid of me that easily. This is a fight I intend to win. And if he even thinks about trying to leave me … well, he's going to damn well tell me to my face.

CHAPTER 23

"I CAN'T BELIEVE *this is happening.*" *Kiki's words came in uneven gasps, forced out past her tears.*

"I have to," he said. "I have to do the right thing."

"You do." Her earnest brown eyes were fixed on him. "Please, Noah, please do the right thing."

She lifted her hand, reaching for him, but he couldn't hold onto her. The diamond engagement ring flashed, and it seemed to him that every sparkle cut him like glass, slicing his hand until it bled.

He tried to hold tight to her hand, but the blood was too slippery. And every time he grasped her, she slipped further away, until they were looking at each other across a wide pool of blood.

Noah woke with a start in the too-soft motel bed. He'd arrived at the rundown motel outside of Oklahoma City yesterday evening, but it had been too late to visit Darla even if he'd wanted to.

He hadn't.

Eventually, yes. Soon, even.

In just a few hours, he'd have to get his head on straight. Then he'd pull on clothes, slip on his shoes. He'd have to go through all the motions of a normal morning on a morning that was the farthest thing from normal. A morning where ghosts and fears and every-thing he thought he'd gotten past were right back beside him again. Telling him he owed her. That Darla was his responsibility, and it was on his head to make it right for her.

And Kiki—oh, dear God, he wanted her beside him. Wanted her hand in his, her strength flowing through him.

But at the same time, he didn't want her seeing him like this. Lost and ripped open. All his old wounds exposed. The guilt that had dulled, now sharp and fresh again.

Guilt for taking Darla to Mexico. For losing her.

And, now that he knew she was alive, the hard, bitter guilt of failure. The raw, painful tearing of his gut, punishing him because he hadn't done enough. Telling him that if he'd spent just a few more hours—tried just a little harder—he would have saved her years ago.

It was true, goddammit. He'd given up. He'd held Diana's tiny body, and he'd been certain that Darla had been murdered, too.

He'd given up, and his wife had suffered.

No way was he making Kiki suffer, too. Because she would. She'd hear what happened to Darla, and every moment would feel real to her. She'd face the existence of a child he had by another woman, and suddenly she'd end up cowering under the weight of the loss and guilt and fucked up emotional mess that had settled on his shoulders once again. A guilt that wasn't hers to bear.

He couldn't be that selfish. He wanted her beside him, yes. But he couldn't have her. And he'd done the right thing by coming to Oklahoma alone. He was certain of it.

That painful reality propelled him off the bed and onto his feet.

Goddammit.

He'd been doing so well. Hell, *they'd* been doing so well. He'd finally got his shit together—finally felt as though he'd earned his right to be with her. And now...

Well, now it felt like he was being punished.

Without letting himself have time to think about it, he grabbed his phone off his dresser, then pressed the button to speed dial Kiki. But he disconnected the call even before the first ring.

He was being selfish. Wanting to hear her voice, even though he knew damn well that he'd hurt her by coming to Oklahoma on his own.

But, dammit, maybe he was just a selfish son-of-a-bitch, because he couldn't stand it.

The phone in his hand seemed to taunt him, and before he could talk himself out of it another time, he called her number again.

His heart pounded in his chest, every cell in his body anticipating her answer—and yet when he finally heard her soft, breathy, "This is Kiki Porter," it wasn't enough because it wasn't really her.

He'd reached her voicemail, and his entire body seemed to deflate.

"Kiki," he said, wishing it truly was her. And, more than that, wishing that she was beside him.

"Kiki," he repeated, "it's me. I—I just want to say that I love you. And I'm so goddamn sorry. But I have to do this. I have to do it alone."

He thought for a moment, wondering if there wasn't something else he needed to say. But there wasn't. Or, rather, he needed to say everything. But how the hell could he do that on a voicemail? For that matter, how could he find the words?

He clicked off without saying goodbye, unable to deal with the finality of even that simple word.

With a sigh, he closed his eyes, replaying her message in his head. Memorizing the sound of her voice, the rise and fall of inflection.

It didn't help. He still felt alone. Hollow.

But he also knew it was time.

He had to go see Darla.

He had to do the right thing.

THE HOUSE SAT small and gray and lonely at the end of a long driveway that cut through the middle of acres of farmland. Noah slouched in his rented Nissan at the intersection of the driveway and the county road and stared at it like something out of a horror movie.

And why not?

He was fucking terrified.

He could turn back, he knew. Tell Darla that she was on her own. Tell Kiki that he belonged to her.

Except he couldn't, not really. He didn't love Darla any more. He wasn't sure he ever really had. But they'd worked to build a life together, and between the two of them, she'd damn sure drawn the short straw.

Forget his guilt. Forget his desperate wish that he could erase the past and start all over again. In the end, none of that mattered. All that mattered was doing the right thing by Darla today. Right now. In this moment.

And that meant turning into the driveway.

The closer he got to the house, the more he could see the deterioration. The siding was coming off, and most of the exterior walls needed painting. The front, however, had been recently spruced up. Fresh flowers in pots, and the simple wooden railing painted in a cheerful blue.

Darla, he thought. Probably with help from her son.

Even as the thought entered his head, a gangly boy with dark hair came barreling around the corner. He wore a simple blue T-shirt and jeans with holes at the knees. He skidded to a halt when he saw the car, and his dark brown eyes went wide.

Noah looked at his face, and his heart flipped over.

The boy turned sharply and barreled up the stairs onto the porch. He yanked open the door, his cry of "Mamá, Mamá," echoing behind him.

Noah parked the car, gathered himself, and walked to the steps.

He was just starting to climb them, when he heard Darla's still-familiar voice from inside the house. "Ricardo Garcia, do we yell in the house?"

Noah couldn't hear the answer, but a moment later she pushed open the screen door, then stepped onto the porch at the same time he reached the top step.

Her eyes widened. In surprise. In joy. Maybe even in fear. He didn't know, and he supposed it didn't matter.

For better or for worse, he was here.

"Noah," she whispered.

"Darla. Oh, God, Darla." His throat was thick. His vision blurry. She was alive—she was really alive.

He'd known it, of course. But seeing it was different, and a whirlwind of emotion swirled inside of him, both wonderful and terrifying.

She hurried to him, obviously intent on throwing her arms around him, then stopped only inches away, her head down, her hands going deep into the pockets of the simple dress she wore.

He took her hands and held them tight in his. He knew she wanted more—a full-on embrace—but this was all he could offer her right now. *Slowly,* he thought. *Right now, he had to move slowly.*

"How?" he said. "How are you here? I thought—I thought you were dead. Diana, she—"

"I know." She blinked, and tears spilled from her pale blue eyes. "They took her. They took us both."

He swallowed, not wanting to hear this, but knowing he had to. "Tell me what happened." His voice was gentle. But also insistent.

With a small nod, she took his hand, then led him to the porch swing. "You don't want to go inside. It's—well, my mother hasn't been well for a while. I'm trying to help her clean it up, but I work a double-shift at the Dairy Queen, and I'm usually too tired to do much cleaning."

She said it casually, and once again he wondered why she'd sought him out. Was it for help? Or was it simply for the connection to someone from her past?

"Outside is fine. Is your son—is Ricardo okay by himself?"

"He's fine. He's a good kid." She drew a deep breath, then dove into her story without warning. "You remember I'd taken Diana out to the market, and we were supposed to meet you later, after you gave that presentation."

It wasn't a question. Of course he remembered that day. It was burned into his memory. "I never saw you again."

"I never saw Diana again," she said, then reached out, took his hand, and squeezed. "I'm so sorry. I'm sorry they took her from me. I'm sorry she—"

"*No.*" His voice was hard. Firm. "Don't do that to yourself. Do you think it was your fault? It wasn't. It was their fault. Whoever they were, they're the ones who did this to her. To us."

The words came out with a fierce intensity, and he meant every one of them. But it was only then—in that moment of speaking them to the woman who'd been his wife, who'd been the mother of his child—that he realized how true they were for him, too. Diana's death wasn't his fault any more than it was Darla's. And whatever hell Darla had experienced wasn't his fault, either.

The revelation felt transcendent, and yet the world remained remarkably mundane. The porch swing creaked. The wind whistled through a nearby elm. And Darla sat beside him, her face sad but hopeful. As if she wanted to believe, but couldn't.

"Go on," he said gently. "Tell me what happened

that day. And then what happened after."

"That's just it—I don't know. All these years, and the only thing I know is that I was wearing the baby sling, and Diana was asleep. I was in the market looking at leather goods. I wanted to get you a wallet. I remember it was very crowded, people bumping into me all the time, and I kept one hand on Diana. I remember I was glad that my money was in my bra, because it would be so easy for someone to pick a pocket in that crowd."

She licked her lips. "I turned toward the noise, and as I did, I felt something sharp prick my arm. I was wearing a sleeveless dress, and I thought I'd brushed against a display rack or something. I remember thinking that I'd need to put some Neosporin on it when we got back to the hotel. And that's it."

"It?"

With a small shrug, she released his hand, then twisted her fingers together in her lap. As she spoke, she looked down at her hands. "That's all I remember. The next memory I have, it was six months later. I was in a hospital. A mental ward. Like something out of one of those horror movies where the people in asylums get free and rampage the town. It was dark and smelled like mildew and the food was never solid, and my first thought was that I was dead. I didn't remember Diana— or find out what happened to her—until much later."

"Darla…" He trailed off. He didn't know what else to say.

"There was a doctor. Enrique Garcia. He was kind to me. He worked with me. Told me that I'd been found in a gutter with a knife wound." She lifted her shirt to reveal a jagged abdominal scar.

"Did he know who you were?"

Darla shook her head. "No. Later I found out we were halfway across the country. So he hadn't heard any reports about my disappearance." She licked her lips. "And he told me that I was pregnant. About six months."

His gut twisted. Their marriage had always felt tentative, but the trip to Mexico was supposed to end at a resort. It was almost supposed to be a second honeymoon. He'd felt like a heel for dragging her to Mexico City first, and he'd surprised her on their second night in town with a candlelit dinner in their room, and they'd made love while the baby slept peacefully in her bassinet.

But he had to ask—of course, he had to ask.

"Did they—when they took you—did they rape you?"

She shook her head. "I don't know. I don't think so. I don't want to think so."

He swallowed, then nodded slowly. He understood her hesitation. She'd had enough horror, why add that violation to the pile? "Eventually you remembered some things. Was that only recently? Before you came to Texas and found me?"

For a moment, he thought she wouldn't answer. Then she lifted her head and faced him. "No." The word was flat. Even. "I worked with Enrique for months after I found myself in that hospital. He took me away to his private facility. And we had long sessions. I—well, it was hard. But he was kind and eventually I started to remember."

"The attack?"

She shook her head. "No. Well, not enough. Just what I described to you. And the fear. I remembered the fear." Once again, she looked down at her hands. "And I remembered them killing Diana. They killed her in front of me. Then they—they tossed her out of a van."

Her voice broke and her body was stiff with an effort at control. Moments passed as she simply breathed. Then she faced him, her chin high. "That's when I remembered you, too."

He frowned, confused. "When was this?"

"About a year and half after I came back to myself."

"That means ... wait. You remembered me over seven years ago?"

Her throat moved as she swallowed. "I didn't tell anyone, not even Enrique. Not for a long time. I was so angry. I blamed you for everything. I remembered losing Diana and I wanted to die. I thought of you, and I wanted you to be the one who died."

He flinched, the emotion in her words more familiar than he cared to admit. But he forced himself to stay level. He needed information to move forward, because none of them could move back. "And all the years between now and then? Where have you been?"

"With Enrique," she whispered. "I lived with him. It was a marriage in everything but the law, because in my heart, I knew I was still married to you. He was a father to Ricardo even though you—well, it doesn't matter. Ricardo believes that Enrique was his dad. And—and despite everything, I was happy."

"And you didn't tell anyone? Not even your mother?"

"No."

"Why not?"

"At first I was too angry. Too lost. I was practically non-functional for years. I wanted to hurt you. And then, when I told Enrique about you and about Diana, he helped me realize that you weren't any more at fault than I was. And by then … well, by then I was happy." She pressed her lips together as she looked at him. "I'm sorry, Noah. I'm so sorry."

Her apology washed over him, and he tried to decide if he was angry or fine or just plain numb. How could he judge her choices after the hell she went through? And at the same time, how could he forgive her for keeping him in hell for all these long years?

He avoided the question altogether by asking, "What happened to Enrique?"

"He died six months ago," she said, and for the first time, tears spilled from her eyes. "His family took everything, and because we weren't legally married, neither Ricardo nor I got anything. His will—he was young. He never got around to putting us in his will."

"And so you came to me…"

"Maybe I don't have any right. It's been so long. But you're still my husband, Noah." Slowly, she reached for his hand. "I'm the mother of your son. And, and I—I'm not angry any longer."

Noah closed his eyes, fighting back a shudder. Fighting back the memories of a day long ago, when she'd told him she was pregnant.

Then, as now, he knew what he had to do.

CHAPTER 24

I T'S JUST BEFORE two when I reach Noah's motel. It's a long strip of rooms with parking in front of each door and an office at one end. The paint is faded from the sun, and the angles seem slightly off, as if a tornado tried to pull it up, but then changed its mind.

It's tidy, though, with potted plants and clean signage, and not a scrap of litter in the parking lot. It's almost friendly. Despite its design, it doesn't have a Bates Motel vibe at all.

I'm hoping that's a good omen. Because I came here searching for a happy ending.

Unfortunately, my hope fades when my knock at number twelve goes unanswered.

I try again. "Noah? Noah, it's Kiki. Can we talk?"

It's futile, of course. I can see that there's no car anywhere near number twelve. Or number eleven or thirteen. None except the rental I grabbed in Oklahoma after my flight landed about an hour ago.

In other words, he's not here.

I draw a deep breath, then let it out slowly, trying to decide what to do. I can wait. Or I can go to Darla's house.

I have the address. Bless Ryan and Dallas, they've both been helping me with this secret mission. In fact, Ryan was the one who not only gave me the address of this hotel, but called the office and told them I was supposed to be a registered guest in the room.

So that's my other option. I can go get my key, then wait in the room.

But if I do that, then I run the risk that he'll have already talked to Darla.

Go to her house, though, and I think I'm crossing some invisible line between stating my case and interfering in the part of his life that doesn't belong to me.

Well, hell.

Ultimately, I decide to pretend like I'm a grown-up. I get the key, I go inside the room, and then I start to pace a hole in the carpet. Because if I stop moving, my mind's going to spin even more. And I'll worry about what they're saying. And then I'll get in my car and race to her house, and I know I shouldn't do that because—

I freeze at the sound of a key in the lock.

The door opens, he steps in, then stops dead when he sees me. "Kiki?"

His expression is flat. Unreadable. And my stomach clenches tight with worry.

"You're an idiot," I blurt, then watch as his eyes go wide and a grin spreads across his face.

"If you mean because I've spent most of the last decade feeling guilty about something I had no control over, then yeah, you're right. I'm an idiot."

"Oh." I hesitate. That wasn't the response I was expecting. "Actually, I meant that you're an idiot for not

259

pulling me into your decisions. You tell me you're going to put a ring on my finger, and then you just leave because you think it will be hard for me to handle? Screw that."

He says nothing, and since I'm on a roll, I continue. "For that matter, I'm an idiot, too. Because I just sat back and let it happen. Well, no more." I take two long steps, then stop right in front of him. "You're mine, dammit. And you are not getting back with Darla. Not without a fight, that's for damn sure. And for that matter, I—what?"

I step back, my eyes narrowed. "You want to tell me why you're grinning."

"This is why," he says, then pulls me close, one arm going around my waist as his other slides into my hair. Then he takes me in a kiss so deep and consuming that I feel the force of it burn through me, making my knees go weak and my core wet and slick with need.

When he finally breaks the kiss, I'm breathless. "Oh," I say. "I should put up a fight more often."

"Everything you said—every single word—all I can say is yes. I love you, baby. I can't do this without you. I don't want to, and I shouldn't have tried."

"You're not getting back together?" I have to lay it out there. I have to make him say the actual words. Because if I'm wrong—if I'm misunderstanding this conversation…

"I'm not with Darla. I'm with you."

"Oh." My legs are like rubber, and I park myself on the edge of the bed. "Thank God."

"She wanted me to," he says, and my stomach

clenches. "I told her no. I told her my fiancée wouldn't approve."

"Fiancée," I repeat. I look at my naked left hand. "You sure about that?"

He takes both my hands in his. "It's seems ridiculously fast, but if you think about all the years put together, it's actually ridiculously slow. And I know I said that we weren't ready yet, but I was wrong. I am ready. I realized it the moment I got here and you weren't by my side. Please, Kiki," he says, sliding off the bed and onto one knee. "Will you marry me?"

I launch myself off the bed and into his arms, then answer him with a bone-melting kiss.

"Is that a yes?" he asks when we come up for air.

"A very enthusiastic one," I confirm. "I love you, Noah Carter. I have for a very, very long time."

He pulls me close again and considering the heat in his eyes, I have no doubt as to his intentions. And even though I want nothing more than to feel his body pressed against mine, I need to know one more thing.

Gently, I press my palm against his chest. "What about your son?"

"He's not my son," Noah says, his brow furrowed. "And I don't think Darla realizes that."

"Are you sure he's not? How do you know?"

"He has brown eyes. Mine are green. Hers are blue. There's no way I'm that kid's father."

My heart wants to leap, but then I realize what that means. "If she got pregnant that close to the kidnapping…"

He nods. "She doesn't remember being raped. And I

think she's blocking the realization of what his eye color means. The man she lived with in Mexico was a doctor. A shrink. But, still, he must have known."

"The man she lived with?" I ask, and he tells me her story. A heartbreaking story of loss and pain and guilt.

"She adores the kid," Noah says. "Honestly, I like him, too. Acknowledging the truth is going to be hard for her."

"What do you want to do?" I ask.

"Help her," he says, the words sounding both simple and extraordinary.

"How?"

"I have some ideas. Financial. And emotional. She's going to need therapy, I think, when she has to let go of the fantasy that I'm Ricardo's father. I thought you and I could talk about all the options. Figure out together what would be best to do for her. And for Ricardo."

Tears prick my eyes. Not just because he wants to help Darla, but because he also wants me at his side, helping him work through this. "Of course," I say. "We'll do it together."

"But not now," he adds with a grin.

"No?" I smile innocently. "Why not."

"There's something else we're going to do now."

"Oh, is there? Making decisions again for me, Mr. Carter?"

He flashes a wicked smile. "Yeah. As a matter of fact, I am."

"Is that so?" I lift a brow. "Then I guess you need to tell me what to do."

"Kiss me," he demands, and I don't hesitate. I turn

so that I'm facing him directly, then hold onto his shoulders as I kiss him deeply, my mouth open, my tongue tasting all of him, this man who is truly mine now. To tempt and explore. Love and hold.

His arms go around me, and he pulls me close, then settles me on his lap so that I'm straddling him, my legs on the bed behind him and my crotch pressed hard against him.

He wrests control from me, deepening the kiss. Claiming me. Marking me.

It's wild. Raw. An assault on my senses, and I feel it all the way down to my core.

"I want you," I murmur, squirming to emphasize the point.

"That's convenient." He gently bites my bottom lip. "Because you have me. Now, and for the rest of our lives."

And that, I think, sounds just about perfect.

EPILOGUE

Six months later

"IT'S MINE? REALLY? You mean it?" Ricardo clutched the acoustic guitar tight and looked up at Noah with a smile so wide it showed off all his teeth. "I get to keep it?"

"It's yours." Noah laughed as the kid squealed "Yes!" then started to strum the guitar while belting out a chorus of *thank you* and *gracias*, slipping seamlessly between his two languages just as he did in regular conversation.

"Hey, hold on." Noah reached for the boy's shoulder, stopping the insanity. "I'm not the one you have to thank. I only asked your mom what you might like for your birthday. She's the one who said a guitar. I didn't even know you played."

"I'm gonna be in a band when I grow up," Ricardo announced. "Just like Kiki." He looked around the yard of the small Tulsa rental house. "Where is she? I need to thank her."

"Come on." Noah nodded toward the front door. "I think she's inside with your mom making sure your *abuela* likes her new bedroom.

The boy raced ahead, and Noah followed, moving swiftly through the three-bedroom house, tidy despite the stacks of boxes.

He found Ricardo in the kitchen, where he was embracing Kiki in a bone-crushing hug, still singing his thank you song.

"Let up there, kid," he chastised. "That's my fiancée you're accosting."

"It's the best present ever," he said sincerely.

"We figured you'd like it," Kiki said, moving to Noah's side and taking his hand.

"Why don't you go sing something for Grandma," Darla said, returning from the back bedroom. "She's resting, and I'm sure she'd love that."

Ricardo nodded, then took off down the hall as Darla smiled at the two of them.

"And now you get my thanks, too," she said.

"Stop it," Kiki said. "You've thanked us so many times I've lost count."

"This house. My tuition. A living allowance. The trust for Ricardo. The doctors, too." She blinked back tears, her eyes going to Noah. "It's too much. And more than you had to do."

He knew what she meant. Ricardo wasn't his son, and they both knew it now. But that didn't mean he was going to back away. Not from her, and not from her son. "We didn't have to do anything," he said gently, squeezing Kiki's hand. Because every dime they'd spent, every decision they'd made, had been done together. "But we wanted to."

Noah had hired attorneys to bring Darla back from

the dead, on paper, at least. Then they'd helped her get enrolled at the University of Tulsa, where she was going to begin in the fall, studying toward a degree in early education.

As for the rest—the medical bills so that she could see a counselor, the allowance so that she could go to school without having to work, the trust to ensure Ricardo's future, and the rental house while she finished school—all of that seemed like a no-brainer. She and Noah might not be married anymore, but she was still his family.

As if following his train of thought, Kiki leaned against him. "We're just glad we can help," she told Darla. "We're all family now. We're happy to do it."

Darla's lips curved up. "Family," she repeated, then reached out to take each of their hands. "It's crazy, but I guess it's true."

"Mom! Come here," Ricardo called, and Darla rolled her eyes.

"I've been summoned. Back in a sec."

"I think crazy's perfectly okay," Kiki said as Darla disappeared down the hall. "I'm crazy about you, after all.""Are you?" he asked, as she twisted in his arms.

"Mmm-hmm." She lifted herself up on her tiptoes. "I'll prove it," she said. And then she closed her mouth over his, capturing him with the kind of kiss that made the world disappear. That made him forget everything except the feel of her in his embrace.

Most of all, it was a kiss with the power to make him certain that no matter what else happened, he was going to spend the rest of his life with the woman he loved.

FOR IMMEDIATE RELEASE
Hardline Entertainment is pleased to announce that Pink Chameleon, the Grammy Award winning band of such hits as *Back to You* and *Turnstile*, will kick off its North American *Back to You* tour with a fundraising performance at the historic Paramount Theater in Austin, Texas.

According to lead singer Kiki King and Hardline CEO Matthew Holt, all proceeds from this first stop on the tour will benefit the Stark Children's Foundation, a nonprofit organization dedicated to helping abused, traumatized, and disenfranchised children.

Noah Carter, the president of Stark Applied Technology Austin and an SCF Youth Advocate, announced that one hundred children currently enrolled in the SCF program will be provided transportation to and VIP seating at the concert, as well as backstage access.

Carter and King recently celebrated their one year wedding anniversary. The couple splits their time between Austin, Texas, and Los Angeles, California.

Brilliant. Charismatic. Sexy as hell.
From the outside, these men seem to have it all.

They don't. They're broken.

And all the money in the world
can't make them whole or buy them love.

That, they'll have to earn.

Broken Billionaires

A new Stark World series
Coming in 2018 from J. Kenner

Only his passion

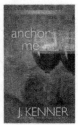

could set her free ...

Meet Damien Stark in the series that started it all ...

The Stark Series
by J. Kenner

Available Now

Happily ever after is just the beginning.

The passion between Damien & Nikki continues.

**Stark Ever After novellas
By J. Kenner**

Available Now

Jackson Steele.
He was the only man who made her feel alive.

Lose yourself in passion . . .

Stark International
By J. Kenner

Available Now

Three powerful, dangerous men ...

Three sensual, seductive women ...

Three passionate romances.

Most Wanted
By J. Kenner

Available Now

It was wrong for them to be together . . .

But harder for them to be apart.

The Dirtiest Trilogy
By J. Kenner

Available Now

Sometimes it feels so damn good to be bad...

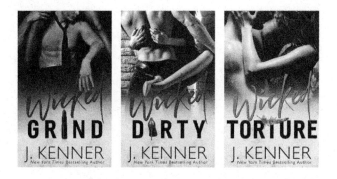

The Wicked Books
By J. Kenner

J. Kenner (aka Julie Kenner) is the *New York Times*, *USA Today*, *Publishers Weekly*, *Wall Street Journal*, and #1 International bestselling author of over eighty novels, novellas and short stories in a variety of genres.

Though known primarily for her award-winning and international bestselling erotic romances, JK has been writing full time for over a decade in a variety of genres including paranormal and contemporary romance, "chicklit" suspense, urban fantasy, and paranormal mommy lit.

JK has been praised by *Publishers Weekly* as an author with a "flair for dialogue and eccentric characterizations" and by RT Bookclub for having "cornered the market on sinfully attractive, dominant antiheroes and the women who swoon for them." JK has been a finalist for Romance Writers of America's prestigious RITA award five times, and a winner once, taking home the first RITA trophy awarded in the category of erotic romance in 2014 for her novel, *Claim Me*.

Before diving into writing full time, JK worked as an attorney in Texas and California where she practiced primarily civil, entertainment, and First Amendment law. She currently lives in Central Texas, with her husband, two daughters, and two rather spastic cats.

Visit her website at www.jkenner.com to learn more and to connect with JK through social media!